You've Got *the* Wrong Number

Aimee Stone

ISBN-13 978-0-9824638-6-4

ISBN-10 0-9824638-6-3

Library of Congress Control Number: 2020918415

Printed in United States of America

Published by BookWorm Publications, LLC

102 W Rockingham Street, #334

Elkton, VA 22827 USA

Visit www.AimeeStone.com

You've Got *the* Wrong Number

Aimee Stone

CHAPTER ONE

HOMECOMING

The big football game is tonight. It's Homecoming weekend and we are up against our rivals, the Hornets. We're the Wildcats and we pride ourselves on our football team. Our whole town does. I go to almost all the games, but my friends and I sit in the most deserted section of the stands. I love seeing the band at halftime as much as the football game. My twin brother, Brian, plays on the football team and our younger sister, Ali, is in the band. I'm the only one that doesn't have something to do on game nights.

I'm not as popular as Brian. Everyone loves him and they always have. He's the definition of the All-American football star. All the guys want to be him, and all the girls want to be with him. Even my best friends crush on him, both of them. I'm not what you would call fat, but I am curvy. James says I'm curvy in all the right places, but he's gay, what does he know about it? I have long dark hair, green eyes and *lots* of curves. Most guys in our school like the thin, blonde hair, blue-eyed, easy girls. Not my brother. He has had the same girlfriend since freshman year. They had a lab together and they've been inseparable ever since. Jenny is perfect. Okay, yes, she has beautiful long blonde hair, brown eyes, she is athletic, and she is a cheerleader but none of that defines her. She is not "easy" like most of the other cheerleaders, or *all* the other cheerleaders. I think the reason some of those girls are so free with their bodies is because they think that it's the only way a boy will like them or show them any attention. If that is the only way to get any attention, then I am happy like this. Boyfriendless, attentionless, and inexperienced in the love department. I am proud to be an eighteen-year-old virgin if giving up my body is what it takes to be popular and have a boy take an interest in me. I will only give myself to someone that I love, not some popularity contest.

My best friends and I are watching the game from our usual spot. James is cheering loudly as he jumps up and down. Brian just made a touchdown, which is no big shock, he does almost every time he touches the ball. His best friend, Jordan, is the quarterback and he throws to Brian a lot. Not just because he's his best friend but because Brian catches everything he is ever thrown. I laugh at James and his antics. Even he has a crush on Brian. My brother knows about the crush that James has, and he teases him that if he ever plans on "batting for the other team" James will be the first one he tells. I think James prays every night that Brian will magically become gay. Even Jenny says if she has to lose Brian, she hopes it would only be to James.

Sadie is my other best friend. She and I love talking about boys. Even though neither of us has ever had an actual boyfriend. She says her first, Clark, doesn't count because they never were boyfriend and girlfriend. Even James gets in on our discussions about boys. He gives us a very different point of view. He says that even though he is gay, and likes dick as much as Sadie, he's still a guy. He says he still thinks like a guy and can tell us what they are thinking. Everyone should have a James. I love him and Sadie. My life would be so boring without them.

"Brandy... did you see that?" James squeals as he grabs my arm, still jumping up and down.

I laugh at his excitement. "I saw, James." I cheer and clap along with them.

"That was awesome! Brian is the best receiver we've ever had," Sadie joins in praising my brother. I just have to laugh as my two BFF's watch my brother as if he's the best thing that has ever graced the walls of our school. It isn't that I don't agree, because he is a great football player, a good friend to all of the school and the best brother I could have ever asked for, but he's just a person like the rest of us.

We ended up winning the game 20-17. There's going to be lots of partying going on tonight. The whole school will be going to one big party. I never really cared about going to parties, but Sadie made me promise that if we won tonight, I would go with her. I guess I'm going to have to pay up tonight.

"Yay! Party tonight!" Sadie yelled as she smiled at me.

I rolled my eyes. "Yeah, I know."

"You girls have fun... I have a date tonight," James announced.

I'm not really surprised. James has had more action than any of us. Sadie has had one guy she messed around with, but they never became actual boyfriend/girlfriend. He was the one she gave her virginity to, but he moved away at the end of our freshman year. I think they'd probably still be together if he hadn't moved but since then she has not dated anyone else. Slept with someone, yes. Dated, no. I've never had a real date. I know... it's hard to believe. My brother is one of the most popular guys in school and I'm his screwed up, shy, virgin sister. Hopefully, college will be better for me in that department.

I see my brother heading over to the cheerleaders before going to the locker rooms. He picks Jenny up, and gives her a kiss on the lips as he spins her around in a circle. He puts her down then looks up into the stands, where he knows we are always sitting. Once he sees us, he waves. Yeah, that's my brother. I love him.

I feel Sadie pulling my arm. "Come on Brandy. We have a party to go to."

Ugh. I really don't want to do this. I don't like big crowds, and I know which party she is talking about. The one where my brother will be. Jordan's party. The only party happening tonight. Jordan is the most popular guy in school. Only beating out Brian because he's the quarterback. I have known him almost my whole life. Jordan and my brother are a lot alike. They're both really good guys. They make good grades, are great on the field and both have dated cheerleaders. The only thing is that Jordan has dated them all, I think. He's what I would call a serial dater. He goes on dates, hooks up, and hangs out with different girls all the time. He doesn't have one girl he sticks with. He isn't a cheater; they all know that he isn't serious with them or going to date just them... and apparently, they are okay with it. Jenny is the only cheerleader he has never been "seen with". At least, not without Brian there, too.

About half an hour later we end up at Jordan's house. He has always invited me to his parties, I'm the other half of Brian, after all. It's just that I don't go. Well, not since the one and only I actually made it to. When we just started our freshman year, Sadie talked me into saying yes to one of his bonfires. His parties were always legit. He has a huge field behind his house where he builds a huge bonfire and that is always the location of his parties.

It was freshman year and Jordan was having his first party of the year. Sadie had talked me into going and James was excited to be included. He was crushing on my brother even back then. Brian didn't care. He thought James was cool and he never judged him for being gay. Jordan hadn't come out to many people back then but Brian knew. I think Jordan did, too. He was cool with James.

There were huge logs set up near the fire and kids all over the place. Football players, both from Jordan and Brian's team, as well as from the Varsity team. Even back then they were popular. Upper-classmen were always at all Jordan's parties. I felt so out of place, but Sadie wanted to talk to a guy that she had met on the first day of school. He was the one that she would later give her virginity to... but that is a story for another day.

The music was playing, the fire was HOT. Some kids were roasting marshmallows, some were playing drinking games, and others were making out. The older kids always brought the alcohol. No one bothered us back there. Jordan had a huge barn that we could use to sleep in if they were too drunk to drive home. Most people stayed. I was not a drinker. I had never gotten drunk before. I don't know what possessed me to drink that night.

I got more than a little drunk that particular night. My judgment was a little impaired... okay, a lot impaired. I would never have fallen for it if I was sober. I got a note passed to me by some kid that I didn't know. He must have been there with someone. It read... "Meet me at the edge of the woods. I have something for you." After I read it, I looked up to ask the kid what this was about and to find out who it was from, but he was already gone. I looked for him, but I couldn't find him. I saw Sadie over by the fire and I went to talk to her. She said that I should go and see who it was from and what they wanted.

She was convinced it was someone that liked me. I wasn't. Against my better judgment, I went.

It was dark by the woods. It was far enough from the fire it was harder to see. Someone came up behind me and put their hands over my eyes. They whispered to me to be quiet. He said that he wanted to talk to me because he liked me, but he didn't want me to know who he was yet. Yeah, I should have run away then. But being intoxicated made me stay. I let him do it. It was the worst decision of my life. He covered my eyes and pressed his body up against my back. I was too busy trying to figure out who it was to notice that his hands weren't the only ones on me. There was someone else in front of me and his hands were on my waist. I wasn't not sure why I didn't know they were there. The one in the front was pressing up against me, too. I can remember parts of it. I remember feeling him hard against me. He was sexually aroused and had started to kiss my neck. It took me a few minutes to realize what was going on. By this time, he already had his hands up my shirt and under my bra. I guess I had been gone too long and James came looking for me. I was so thankful that he did. When he called out my name, the boys let me go and James found me with my shirt up around my neck, my jeans unfastened and part of the way down my thighs.

I hate to think about what would have happened to me if he hadn't come looking for me. I haven't been to a party since that night, I was too scared to go. I never did find out who the two boys were. I'm not even sure that there were only two of them… I was afraid I would see them again and that they would try to finish what they started. Parts of that night have come back to me and others haven't. I'm glad that I don't remember all of it. I'd be fine with that small part of my life staying buried.

When we get to the party, I see kids all around. There are trucks with their tailgates down, some holding coolers, some providing seats. The fire is large and I can see the bright orange sparks rising up from the top of the flames. I hear the crackling of the wood as it burns, and the smell is strong. I've always loved the smell of a fire, we have them when we go camping, which is all the time. This is just on a much larger scale, both in terms of fire and guests.

I never told Brian or Jordan what happened that night. James knew and I told Sadie, too, after she kept trying to get me to go to more of Jordan's parties. I finally had to tell her why I just couldn't go. She understood and I understood why she wanted to go... and went to a bunch of them. One of his parties was actually where she slept with Clark the first time. She wasn't drunk and it wasn't forced, so it was different from my first and last party experience. Since Clark moved away, she has been to a few but I still hadn't been able to show up here. I don't know why I agreed to come tonight.

I just hope that I don't regret it.

CHAPTER TWO

THE AFTER PARTY

I'm still standing beside Sadie's car, looking around at all the party kids. She comes over and stands beside me.

"Come on Brandy." She puts her arm in mine. "I promise I won't leave you."

"Thanks."

I know she means it. She knows how hard being here tonight is for me, but I am here. I see Brian and Jenny. Jenny waves as she leaves Brian's side and comes over to Sadie and me. She hugs me instantly.

"I'm so glad you're here. Come on. There's room for both of you with us," Jenny says as she grabs my hand and pulls me with her. Sadie laughs and follows behind us.

"Hey, sis. I didn't expect to see you here tonight," he says as Jenny takes her place back between his legs that are dangling off his tailgate.

"I made her come," Sadie boasts.

I roll my eyes at her. She just smiles and grabs a drink from the table beside Brian's truck. She hands me one, as well. I take a small sip of the golden liquid in the red plastic cup.

"Hey, girls. Glad to see you made it tonight." I hear Jordan's voice from the side of Brian's truck. He comes around to the table and grabs himself a drink. One of the cheerleaders is hanging all over him. That must mean she is going to be his hook-up tonight. Jordan is tall, he must be at least 6' 2". His hair is dark, almost black. He has facial hair that he keeps trimmed down close to his face so it looks like he has a constant 5 o'clock shadow. His eyes are dark blue, and he has the perfect smile, dimples included. He's almost 18-years-old. I can see why every girl in our school and some neighboring schools want to get a hold of Jordan. They all want him to finally choose them to date exclusively but I don't ever see that happening. He says he likes being single and not having anyone to have to answer to.

"Hey, Jordan," Sadie smiles as the blonde girl hanging on his arm gives us both a dirty look. If she only knew... I have already seen Jordan naked. Of course, we were seven and it was when he lost his shorts while we were playing in the water hose in the front yard, but it counts. He was the only boy I have ever seen naked, but I'm for sure not the only girl to have seen Jordan naked. Even though I was the only girl to see seven-year-old Jordan naked.

"Hi, Jordie." I always call him that, even though I know it pisses him off at times. He must be in a good mood tonight because he just laughs. The blonde just stares at me. I can't remember what her name is, not that it matters.

"Can we go now, Jordie?" she says as her grip tightens on his arm. He looks at her and he looks aggravated.

"Don't call me that, Calissa."

She looks at him like he slapped her in the face. "She just did," she says as she looks at me.

"And she is the only person allowed to call me that."

If looks could kill... well, let's just say it would be my funeral. Sadie laughs. Even she doesn't call him Jordie. No one else does. I only do it because I can. I tease him and tell him it was because I was the first to see his *wee-wee*. Yeah, we were seven. It was a *wee-wee*.

"Why can she and I can't?" She says as she pouts.

I just laugh. I can't wait to see if he tells her the reason I always tell him.

His face turns red as he looks at her and says, "Because she was the first to see my *wee-wee*."

All around Brian's truck, people start laughing. I think Brian just might fall off, he is laughing so hard. All of us know the reason but I don't think any of us were expecting him to say it. Especially not using *wee-wee* to describe it. I'm not sure the girl, Calissa I think he called her, is impressed because she turns around in a huff and stomps off towards another group.

"Well, fuck," Jordan says as he runs his hand through his hair.

"Sorry, Jordan." I really am sorry if I ruined his night, but that girl was just horrible.

"Eh, don't worry about it. It would have been hard to spend much more time with her anyway. She's just too damn stupid."

We all laugh again.

We spend the next hour all hanging out. A few more of the football players came over to say hello.

One in particular, has spent a little longer at our group. His name is Christian Harper. He's another one of the stars of the team. He hangs out with my brother and Jordan a lot. He comes by the house all the time to see

Brian and is always super nice. I don't see him spending much time with the skanky girls. If he does, he keeps it more of a secret than the rest do. There have been rumors he's gay, but I don't think he is. Not that it would matter. He's a super nice guy and I enjoy talking to him.

"Good game, Christian," I say when he gets close enough that I can speak to him.

"Thanks, Brandy. You look pretty tonight," he says as he smiles at me.

Sadie nudges my arm. She obviously heard what he said. She says I should go out with him but honestly, I'm not interested. I don't know why. He's super sweet and is really cute, but I just don't have those kinds of feelings. It's not him. I don't want to date any guy.

"Thanks, Christian." I manage to say as I blush. Even though I'm not interested in him like that, I still blush when he compliments me.

"Dude... stop hitting on my sister. It's creepy," Brian says, pushing on Christian's arm.

"You can't keep everyone away from her forever, you know?" Christian responds.

"Maybe not, but I can keep **you** away from her **tonight**."

Christian shakes his head and goes to walk away. Before he leaves, he turns to look at me again. "Whenever your brother decides to stop being such a prick... let me know." He winks at me with a genuine smile on his face before he walks away.

I'm not sure what that's all about. I'll have to remember to ask Brian about it tomorrow. Who all has he kept away from me? What was Christian talking about? Do I want Brian to keep Christian away from me?

We spend another hour talking and laughing. Some of

us even dance. A good song comes on and I can't help but get a little sexy with Sadie.

Hey Sexy Lady - by Shaggy is playing out of someone's stereo speakers. I'm dancing behind Sadie. I grab onto her hips as she rolls them. I press up against her back and run my hands up and down her sides. She knows exactly what I'm doing. She just smiles as she bends down in front of me, pushing her ass back. I smack it as she giggles. She stands up again slowly as I walk around to stand in front of her, trailing my hand around her back and arms until I get around to her stomach. Both of us are moving our bodies slow and sexy. I put my hands on her arms and run them down to her hands.

I run them down her body as I bend my knees and squat down. My hands travel down her sides, down her legs and back up again. I poke my ass out as I come back up her body. She has her hands in her hair, as she rolls into me. She turns around again so that her back is against my front. She leans back so that she's pressed against me. She raises her hands that are still in her hair. She lets go and her long red hair falls over me. By now the song is finishing. We stop dancing and I can see we have gained a few more in our group. All guys.

"Holy fuck," I hear Jordan say as he's looking us both up and down. There's a look in his eyes that I have never seen before.

"What the fuck was that?" I hear Christian ask from behind me. I turn around and see him standing close to me. I hear Jenny giggling. She can see what just happened to the surrounding boys. A couple of them have their mouths hanging open and a few get slapped by the girls beside them.

"Dancing," I say as I smile at Christian. I'm just slightly drunk tonight.

"That was hot as shit," he says. He has the same look in his eyes that I noticed Jordan had when I looked at him.

I smile at him as another song starts playing. *Glamorous* by Fergie is playing. It's a song I know well. I love it and always have to sing, or should I say shout, to it.

I can't help but move when I hear it. "If you ain't got no money take your broke ass home," Sadie and I yell as Ludacris says it at the beginning of the song. "G-L-A-M-O-R-O-U-S" we sing with Fergie. Christian is still standing in front of me. I grab his hand and pull his body closer to me.

"Dance with me." I don't ask him, I tell him. I don't think he minds, though, by the smirk on his face and the way his eyes travel my body.

I start moving to the beat against him. He only takes a few seconds to grab onto me. He smiles as he starts to move to the beat with me, holding my hips. Both my upper body and my hips are rolling around in circles. He turns me around as my body moves and he presses up against my back. His hands move around to my stomach. He's grinding his body on me at this point. I don't think that Christian is gay because I can feel him hard against my ass. But I can't say that I care. Being tipsy has made me not care and I'm loving being in his arms. I'm enjoying that I'm turning him on. He can move well. He's not stiff in his movements at all. The only part of him that is stiff... is the hardness that is currently poking my ass. I'm sure he could rock a girl's world easily. I can hear Sadie and Jenny cheering me on. My brother does not sound impressed as I hear him groan.

"My God, Brandy... you are sexy as fuck," Christian

says as he buries his face in my neck. He places a small open-mouthed kiss there as he grinds his erection into my ass.

"If you ain't got no money, then take your broke ass home," we all yell when it comes on over and over again at the end of the song, with my hands pumping up into the air over my head.

A few more songs played that Christian and I danced to. I was having a good time dancing with him. He was a little handsy with me but not too bad. I didn't mind it at all, I kind of liked it. During one song his hands ventured to my ass as he pulled me into him. My brother saw that one because I heard Brian cough when he did it. A few times I felt Christian's lips on my neck, his breath warm against my skin.

We just finished a song and I need a drink.

"I need something to drink," I say as I pull away from Christian.

He reluctantly lets me go. I go over to the table and grab a beer out of the cooler that's underneath. I needed something cold to cool off both from the dancing and the close body contact going on with Christian. As I take a drink, I see Brian and Jenny making out on the bed of the truck. I see Sadie talking with some guy and I notice Jordan is staring at me. I decide I should apologize to him for causing his date to disappear. I walk over to where he is standing.

"Hey, Jordie."

He laughs.

"I'm sorry that I ran your date off. I didn't mean to," I say. I mean it, I didn't mean to chase her off, even though she was nothing more than a quick lay.

He shrugs his shoulders. "Don't worry about it. She

wasn't that much fun anyway," he laughs. He grabs my beer and takes a drink before handing it back to me.

"I can get you one," I say as I take my beer back.

"Nah... I will just share yours," he says as he takes it back and takes another drink.

I laugh at him. I see the look in his eyes again. The same one that was there earlier.

"That was some dancing you did there." He smirks at me as his eyes travel down my body again. Most people probably wouldn't even notice it, but I know him. I notice everything he does when he's around.

"I'm not sure my brother approved," I say as I look over at him and Jenny kissing.

"Yeah, well... it was pretty sexy."

"It was just dancing," I say, trying to downplay the events of the evening.

Jordan nods over to Christian. "You sure he knows that?"

CHAPTER THREE

THE FIRST TEXT

I'm sure he knows. Well, I'm pretty sure he knows... It was just dancing. Right? UGH, men.

"Yeah," I answer. I'm not sure if I'm telling him or myself that Christian knows it was just some dancing fun.

Jordan looks over at Christian again. "Well, we're just standing here, talking, sharing a beer," he says as he holds the beer up to his lips, "And he looks like he wants to kill me for just being this close to you."

Jordan leans in a little closer to me. Damn, he smells good. "Yeah... there it is... he wants to smash my face in for getting this close to you," he says as he leans closer still.

I turn to look over to where Christian is standing. The look on his face is not what I expected to see. Jordan leans in closer to my ear. He whispers, "Is he twitching yet?"

I quickly turn my head to look at Jordan. In doing so,

my lips touch his. Jordan instantly grabs my face and presses his lips to mine even more. I pull back from him.

Jordan laughs. "Well, I'm sure that did it."

"What the hell, Jordan?" I ask as I pull back from him further.

"What?" he smirks. "You kissed me."

I'm angry now. "I did no such thing."

"I'm pretty sure I felt your lips on mine."

"It was an accident and you know it," I say as I push him back from me. I didn't realize exactly how close he was standing to me.

"Maybe... but can I just say... your lips are soft," he laughs again.

"Ass," I say as I walk away from him. I find my way back to where Sadie is sitting.

"What the hell was that?" Sadie asks me as I take a seat beside her.

"I don't know what you're talking about," I say as I take a drink of the new beer I grabbed on the way to my seat.

"Yeah... right..." She raises her eyebrows at me. "First you get Christian all hot and hard. And then you kiss Jordan? Two football hotties in one night? Damn girl," she laughs again.

"It was just dancing."

"And the kiss?" she asks.

"Accident," I state. I'm still not sure if it's for me or her to make sure to say it was an accident. I take another sip of the beer I'm holding. I need to be a little more tipsy.

"Yeah, I hate when that happens... when my lips happen to touch a football player." She pauses for effect. "One that is hot as hell, I might add."

I take another long drink of my beer, ignoring her comment. She just smiles at me. But she's right. Dancing with Christian was hot. I liked the way his arms felt around me. I liked that dancing with me was turning him on. It was hot. She's also right about the kiss, but don't tell her I said so. It was quick and not what I would consider a real kiss, but damn it was hot. He could also rock a girl's world pretty easily. I don't know what is happening to me tonight. I've never had two guys acting like this... like ever. Tomorrow things will go back to normal and tonight will just be a fond memory. One that I may have to replay in the future.

The rest of the evening is pretty uneventful. We all drink some more; dance some more and just hang out. I don't dance with Christian again like we were earlier. And Jordan no longer has his lips on mine. Both of these boys are like family. We've all known each other since kinder-garten. They have never shown me any interest, of any kind, for our whole lives. It was just the dancing and the drinking that made this happen tonight. It will be forgotten with the morning sun.

I was going to be spending the night with Sadie, but we both are too drunk to drive to her house. We decide we're going to take advantage of the barn and sleep it off. There are several people with the same idea. The barn is pretty nice. It's a horse barn and there are stalls down both sides. Each of the stalls has several inches of pine shavings. There's an area at one end that has bales of hay and where the hay comes loose from the bales, there is a nice area to sleep. Jordan always keeps blankets in the barn's tack room for occasions like this. Sadie and I grab a blanket and we go to one of the stalls. We preferred to have the privacy it provides. They used to all house horses but there are only two here now.

"I'm glad you came with me tonight," Sadie says as we make a bed for us to get some sleep.

"Me, too. I did have a good time," I say as I smile at her. It's true, though. I actually did have a good time.

We get quiet as we hear someone walking down the center aisle. It sounds like two people, actually. I sure hope they aren't coming in here to hook up and we have to hear them. It doesn't take long to hear it is Christian and Jordan.

We should let them know that we're here, but they are already talking.

"What the fuck man?" We hear Christian say.

"What, Chris?" Jordan asks, seeming annoyed.

"What was with that kiss?"

"What kiss?"

"You know what fucking kiss, Jordan." Christian's voice is getting a little raised.

"It was an accident."

"Yeah, sure it was. I saw the way you were looking at her tonight. Don't be an ass, Jordan. She isn't one of your fucks."

Damn, I think they are talking about me. Now I know I can't say anything and let them know I've heard this much of their conversation.

"I know she isn't. I told you. It was an accident," Jordan says again, more aggravated this time. "She turned and... well... we kissed."

"And you just happened to grab her and kiss her more?"

"She had soft lips," Jordan says as he chuckles. "But then, you'd know that if you ever got out of your own fucking way long enough to make a move, wouldn't you?"

"Fuck you." Christian is even more angry. "You know her brother would kick my ass."

"Then drop it. If you're too scared to make a move

because her brother might get pissy... then don't complain when she kisses someone else."

"Thought you said it was an accident?" Christian says with an attitude.

"Fuck off, you pussy."

"Stay away from her Jordan."

I can't believe what I'm hearing. Brian would kick his ass if he talked to me. Why? He has a girlfriend and has for years. Why is it okay for him and not me? I hear another guy entering the conversation now. It sounds like one of the other players.

"Well if neither of you are going to go for it, I will. She is fine as fuck and that dancing. Holy hell she was hot. I don't know how you didn't bend her over right there and fuck her with her all up on your dick," the mystery man says.

I hear Jordan chuckle as Christian answers, "Stay the fuck away from her, David."

It must be David that laughs. "I hear ya man. But if you aren't going to partake in the fine ass that is Brandy... then, by all means, move aside and let one of us have a shot at her."

They've moved on down to the end of the barn now. Sadie and I just look at each other.

She whispers to me, "What the hell was that?"

I whisper back, "I don't know. I think they're drunk."

She giggles. "Oh, they are, but you got three football players wanting... what did he say?" she pauses. "*To partake in, the fine ass that is Brandy*." She laughs again.

I smack her on the arm. "Shut up."

We both laugh.

I know we heard correctly, but they didn't intend for me to hear this conversation. I'm not even sure I wanted to hear this conversation. I know who David is but he is even worse of a player than Jordan is. He's definitely someone that would get his ass kicked by my brother and he would probably deserve it. I know that I enjoyed dancing with Christian. He can move, that's for sure. But I never thought of him like that. Before tonight I wasn't sure he was even straight. Then there's Jordan. I have always thought he was cute and kind of had a small crush on him when we were young, but I never thought of us being together. I'm a shy virgin and he is... well he's not.

Sadie and I get comfortable and cover up with the blankets. I don't know where the guys went. We can't hear them any longer. We talk a little while longer and I'm getting sleepy. I'm just about to go to sleep when my phone vibrates. I pick it up and look at the screen. I see a text message from an unknown number.

> *Him: Hi, beautiful.*
> *Me: Who is this?*
> *Him: A secret admirer.*
> *Me: I think you've got the wrong number.*
> *Him: No, I don't.*
> *Me: Yeah, I'm sure you do.*
> *Him: No, I don't.*
> *Me: Then who is it that you are trying to text?*
> *Him: You.*
> *Me: G'night. Maybe you can check the number again in the morning and get the right person.*
> *Him: I have the right person.*
> *Me: Who is this?*
> *Him: I told you. A secret admirer. You are a good dancer.*

"Who is that?" Sadie asks as she reads over my shoulder. I shrug my shoulders.

> *Him: Where did you go?*
> *Me: Look, I don't know who this is, but you've got the wrong number.*

Him: I promise you, I don't. Your friend is a good dancer, too, but the way you move... damn girl, you have some seriously sexy moves.

Me: I'm going to sleep now.
Him: Goodnight, beautiful.
Me: Night.
Him: Talk to you tomorrow.

I don't answer the last one. I don't know what to say. This is just some drunken text message that will be straightened up in the morning when he can actually read the number he was putting into his phone and he realizes his mistake. He never said anything that proved he knew who he was talking to. There were many of us girls dancing tonight. It could be anyone he was trying to text.

"I don't know who it was. I imagine he will figure it out in the morning that he was drunk texting the wrong person."

"Yeah, maybe," she says as she takes my phone and reads the messages again. "But he seems to think he has the right person."

"And if he was here tonight, he's also drunk right now."

"I guess you'll find out when he texts you again tomorrow," she says with a smirk on her face.

"Whatever." I just want to go to sleep and pretend this didn't happen. Maybe it will be something funny to laugh about tomorrow.

CHAPTER FOUR

THE FIRST TEXT II

The next morning, I wake up and look around. I have shavings in my hair and stuck to one side of my face. I clean my face off and sit up. Sadie is still asleep next to me. I look at my phone to see what time it is. I see there is another text message on my phone from the same unknown number.

Him: Good morning, beautiful. Hope you slept well last night and don't have too bad of a hangover this morning.

I can't help but smile at the message. I see it was sent about an hour ago. I decide I'll send one back to him.

Me: You've got the wrong number. Have a nice day.

Him: ...

He's replying.

Him: I assure you; I have the right number.

I don't know what else to say to this guy. I don't know who he is, and he won't understand that he is texting the wrong girl.

Me: So, let's assume that you do know who you are talking to. Why me?

Him: Are you serious?

Me: Yes.

Him: Why not you?

Me: I'm not popular.

Him: Eh... it's overrated.

Me: Says someone that clearly is.

Him: Would that bother you?

Him: If I was popular?

Me: I don't guess so.

Him: OK, so what else you got as to why not you?

I don't know if I should bring up the way I look or not. I have never cared I was curvy, I actually kind of like my curves, but boys don't seem to.

Me: I'm not pretty.

Him: You're right, you aren't.

Ass.

Him: You are GORGEOUS!!!

Me: See, now I know you don't know who you are talking to.

Him: I do know. I also know what it looks like when you let go and dance like no one is watching.

What do I say to that? I did dance like no one was watching... and then like every guy at the party was watching. And I was enjoying turning them on, especially the one whose arms I was in. What does that say about me?

Him: You still there?

Me: Yes.

Him: Thank you for writing me back this morning. I wasn't sure you would.

Me: Why not? Are you an ogre or something?

Him: Something...

He's funny.

Me: I only wrote you back to tell you, you had the wrong number again.

Him: You sure are stuck on that, aren't you?

Me: I am.

Him: Why?

Me: Because...

Him: I'm waiting...

Him: Patiently...

Him: <<Stomping his foot with arms crossed, waiting>> LOL ;)

Me: So, since you say you know who I am, why text?

Him: I do know who you are. You are the most incredible girl I have ever met. You are beautiful, smart, funny, have killer dance moves and... the most gorgeous green eyes I have ever seen.

Me: How did you know I have green eyes?

Him: I told you, I know who you are.

Me: And who are you?

*Him: In good time you will know. For now, I can be SAM (Your **Secret AdMirer**) and you are the woman I desire. The woman that I dream about. The one that drives me crazy.*

Yeah, I'm not answering that one. I'm not sure how I feel about a guy telling me these things when I don't even know who he is. He could be anyone. There were probably fifty or more people at that party last night. Seniors all the way down to freshman. Popular football players and people I have never seen before.

*Me: Okay, **Sam**... You never answered my question.*

Sam: I thought I did.

Me: Why text? If you are popular and so sure you know who I am, and you want me... why not say this in person and not through text?

Sam: ...

I see the dots appear, disappear, reappear and again they are gone. What is he up to?

Sam: Because I know you. You have never had a real boyfriend. I have never even known you to date. So, I assume for a guy to get your attention, he will have to be special. Just coming up to you and asking you out, that isn't good enough for you. You deserve special and I want you to get to know me. The REAL me before I ask you in person.

Hmm... He's right about that. I'm not sure I would say yes to anyone that I know. I'm not sure if I want a relationship or not. The guy would have to be pretty special to get past all the walls I built up over the years.

"Hey, what are you doing?" Sadie asks as she rubs her eyes.

"Texting Sam."

"Who's Sam? Is there a fifth guy?" she asks with a huge smile.

"No. He said he is my secret admirer, my SA and just added the M."

"I wonder if that's a hint?" she asks as she reads the texts over my shoulder. "So, he wants you to get to know the real him before he meets you in person?"

"That's what he says."

"Cool," she smiles.

My phone vibrates again.

Sam: You still there?

Me: Yeah, my friend just woke up.

Sam: Oh, okay, I will let you go for now.

Me: Okay, have a good day.

Sam: You, too. Tell Sadie I said hello. ;)

"Damn," I say as I read that last sentence.

"What?" she squeals as she grabs my phone. She starts typing.

Me: (Sadie) This is Sadie... you hurt her, and I will kill you.

Sam: Morning, Sadie. I wouldn't dream of ever hurting her. She has all the power to do the hurting here.

Me: (Sadie) Just you remember that!

Sam: I will, I promise. Now, you two need to get out of that stinky barn before the others wake up.

Me: (Sadie) How'd you know?

Sam: I saw you both sleeping in the stall last night and this morning before I left.

Me: (Sadie) Stalker?

Sam: No. Just looking out for her.

Me: (Sadie) You like her, don't you?

"What is he saying?" I ask trying to take my phone back. She swats at my hand and keeps typing.

Sam: Yes, I do. It was all I could do not to come in there and hold her in my arms all night. I wanted to kiss her good night.

Me: (Sadie) Okay, maybe you're alright.

Sam: Thanks, Sadie. Tell my girl I will text her later. Okay?

Me: (Sadie) Will do.

Sadie hands my phone back to me. I read through their messages. "He wanted to hold me last night. And kiss me?"

"Apparently," she says with a smile on her face. She looks around. "I agree, let's get out of this barn." We both laugh.

"His girl?" I say as I read that message again.

"Yeah, he seems smitten with you."

"Smitten?" I ask as I laugh. "Who even says that anymore?

"Well, me, of course." She laughs.

We get up, fold up the blankets and put them away. I see one of the horses with their heads over the barn door and I have to walk up and say hi to him. He's a solid palomino horse with a big white blaze down the middle of his face. He's such a sweet horse.

He nuzzles up to me and I love on his big face. He is such a sweet boy. "Hi, Buddy."

"Should I be jealous of my horse getting more action than I do?" I hear Jordan say as he's laughing behind me.

I jump, "Shit, Jordie. You scared me." I take a breath, "You do know he's cuter than you, right?"

He laughs again. "Sorry, I didn't mean to. I was coming to take him for a ride."

I pet him some more as he sniffs my pockets to see if I have any treats for him. Jordan hands me a piece of peppermint.

"What? My breath stink?" I say covering my mouth with my hand.

He laughs, "No, give it to the horse."

"Oh," we both laugh again as I feed the piece of peppermint to Buddy.

"You want to go for a ride? I can saddle up Bailey, too?" he asks as he pets Buddy on the neck.

"Really? I love horses." I'm getting excited at the thought of going for a ride with Jordan on his horses.

"Sure," he says as he smiles.

We hear a cough.

"Hey," Sadie says as I see her smiling.

"Oh, yeah, I forgot, I didn't drive here last night."

Jordan is putting the halter on Buddy as he talks, "I can take you home."

"I... I don't know."

I see Sadie smiling at me. She is nodding her head yes when Jordan is looking away from me. She nudges my arm towards Jordan. I know what she's thinking. She wants me to try and find out if he is Sam. I just want to go for a ride.

"Sure, I guess," I say quietly.

Jordan smiles. "Good, I'll get her." He takes off into the field and calls for Bailey. She sees us and comes running. He ties her to get her tacked up and ready to ride. Sadie told me to try and figure out if he's Sam. I don't know how to go about that, but I'll try.

Once both horses are saddled, we're ready to go. Jordan helps me up onto Bailey and we take off. It's pretty on his farm. We ride out by where the bonfire was. All the trucks and cars that were in the field are gone. Most of the trash is in the barrels that are placed throughout the area. It looks a lot different during the daylight.

"It's pretty out here. It's harder to appreciate in the dark."

Jordan chuckles. "It is." We ride a little longer before he speaks again. "Why do you call me Jordie?"

"Because I saw your…" he interrupts me.

"Yeah, I know..."

I can see him thinking. "You know, it is much bigger now... I could show you," he pauses, "so you could feel like I earn the upgrade to Jordan."

I laugh. "Nah, I'm good. I'm sure it's much bigger now, but I still prefer *little* Jordie."

We both laugh before he says, " When you change your mind, the offer still stands."

My face turns red and we go back to riding, quietly. The rest of the ride is good. He doesn't bring up showing me his upgraded *wee-wee* anymore and I can't help but wonder if he is Sam. It's obvious I'm not getting that answer today.

After the ride, Jordan takes me home. We get to my house and he walks me to the door.

"You could have just dropped me off."

"Yes, I could have," he says as he leans in.

Is he going to kiss me? Do I want him to? Is he Sam? Do I want him to be Sam? I think I only want Sam to kiss me.

He hugs me and kisses my forehead. "It was great to ride with you. It was a lot of fun. We should do it again sometime."

"Yeah." I look down nervously.

He notices, "What's wrong?" He touches my face. "Is it about that kiss last night?"

I nod.

"I won't kiss you again, until you ask me to." He smiles at me as he glances at my lips. "But as soon as you ask, I will do it again, and I promise you will like it."

I don't know what to say. So, I blurt out the first thing that comes to mind. "Bye." I quickly open the door, run inside and close it. I hear him laughing on the other side before he leaves.

Damn... He could be Sam...

CHAPTER FIVE

THE PLAN TO CATCH SAM

The rest of the weekend was quiet. I texted Sam some more. Sadie came over and we did some homework.

"So, he said he wanted to kiss you?" she asks about Jordan.

"I guess," I say as I shrug my shoulders. "He said he would when I asked him to."

"Do you think he's Sam?" she asks as she twirls her hair in her fingers. She always does this when she's thinking.

"I don't know. I can't imagine anyone being Sam." It's true, I can't picture anyone I know as Sam. It's almost like Sam is a new person, one I don't yet know. But he says he already knows me, so I guess I have to wait and see.

Monday morning is here, and I don't want to get up. I stayed up texting Sam last night. We talked about the football game and the party afterward. He was always careful not to give away too much. I found out his favorite color is red, and he loves camping and being outdoors. We both love horses. We seem to have a lot in common. I guess I could try to find out who all likes these things, as well, but I think they all do.

Sadie says we can narrow it down to Jordan, Christian, and David. I think the reason she thinks that is just because of the conversation we overheard.

I ride to school with Brian and Jenny as usual. "This weekend was a lot of fun, don't you think, Brandy?" Jenny asks with a big smile.

"Yeah, it was," I answer, not wanting to talk about it in front of Brian. I might tell Jenny about the texts but not with Brian here. She would have to swear to secrecy because he would not like it at all.

Once at school, I meet up with Sadie at our lockers. They are right beside each other. I see James coming down the hall. After I talked to Sam last night, I had a three-way call with Sadie and James. We caught him up on what happened at the party and about Sam. He says he thinks it's Jordan from how he acted when we went riding together. I'm not convinced. The day goes by quickly. I see Jordan, Christian, and David but that isn't abnormal. I see them all daily. They're always around Brian and we have classes together.

Sam: Hey, beautiful. You are pretty today.
Me: What?
Sam: I said... you look pretty today. I love what you did with your hair.

I pulled my hair to one side today and put it in a ponytail. It isn't something I often do.

Me: Really?
Sam: Yes. I was unable to focus in class today, though. I just wanted to kiss your neck. Is that bad?

WHAT??

Me: We have a class together?

Sam: Yes, more than one. And I'm having a hard time... lol

I think he just made a sex joke. Or at least a hard on joke. I'm going to have a little fun with this one. I think I'm due. I hand my phone over to Sadie. We are currently at lunch and I'm thinking he is, as well.

"What? This boy has it pretty bad," she says as she hands my phone back to me.

"I think we should have a little fun," I say with a huge smile on my face.

"OH, I love the way you think." We both giggle as I type.

Me: What's hard?

I pause before sending the next message. I see the ... from him.

Me: Hard time with what?

Before I can get my second message sent one comes from him at the same time.

Sam: Currently, I am.

Sadie giggles as she reads his message. "Girl, does he know... you know?"

"That I'm a virgin?" I say in a whisper.

She nods.

"I don't know. He said he knows I've never had a real boyfriend."

"That doesn't mean he knows the other thing," she says as she twirls her hair again.

"What?" I ask her, knowing she is plotting something.

"We need a plan. A plan to figure out who this mystery man is," she says as she looks around to make sure no one is looking.

I laugh, "What do you suggest? Should I see which guy currently has an erection?"

She laughs. "Well, that would work... but I was thinking

more along the lines of me watching one of them while you are texting and see if they are texting, too. We could at least rule out someone like that." I hate to admit it, but she has a good idea. Maybe we should.

"How do we do that?"

"I will hang out with one of them and if Sam texts you and the one I'm with doesn't... we can rule him out," she smiles, proud of herself.

Sam: You still there? I didn't scare you off, did I? Because if I did, I'm sorry.

Me: No, you didn't. I'm still here.

Sam: Good. I'm hoping that pretty smile on your face right now is because of me. ;)

Me: You can see me now?

Sam: Yes. Hence the "hard" time.

I look up and look around the cafeteria. I see David and Jordan over with Brian. They are both on their phones. That doesn't help. However, I don't see Christian.

Me: You can see me right now?

Sam: Yes.

Me: What am I doing now?

I put my finger on my nose like I am going to pick my nose.

Sam: LOL. I didn't know you picked your nose.

Me: Stop it! I just wanted to make sure you weren't lying.

Sam: I would never do that to you.

Me: Then who are you?

Sam: Good try. I said I wouldn't lie, but never said I would tell you who I am... yet.

Me: But you will?

Sam: Yes.

Me: Okay.

Sam: Okay.

We text a little while longer. He can see me. I don't see

Jordan and David anymore and I never saw Christian at lunch today. He must have had something else to do.

> *Sam: I will talk to you tonight, beautiful.*
> *Me: Okay.*
> *Sam: I think we should meet at the Halloween party. We could have on costumes. I would like to touch you.*
> *Me: You would tell me who you are that night?*
> *Sam: Maybe.*
> *Me: Okay.*

I tell Sadie that we have two weeks to figure out who this guy is because I just agreed to meet up with him at the Halloween party.

That afternoon after school, Sadie comes over and we make plans on how she can get with one of them the next day at school. We decided it should be at lunch, since that was when he was texting me today.

The next day seems to take years to get to lunchtime. We told Jenny about what was going on. She said that she wanted to help us find out who it was because she loves a good mystery and a love story and apparently, we have both. I made her promise not to tell Brian. I would later, but there isn't anything to tell now. It probably isn't one of his friends, anyway.

I go to the library during lunch and Sadie goes with Jenny to sit with her and watch the guys. She sends me a text to tell me that the only one at the table right now is Jordan and he isn't on his phone.

It's game time... I have to text Sam.

> *Me: Hey. What are you up to?*

No response.

> *Me to Sadie: I texted him. No response.*
> *Sadie: Jordan isn't on his phone. It's in his pocket. I can't even see if it lit up or not with a message.*
> *Me to Sadie: I am going to call it.*

Sadie: Brave move. Do it.

I call the number that shows up on my phone. It goes to a voicemail that just lists the number and says they are busy. No voice. He's too smart.

Sadie

I'm trying to help my best friend figure out who this is. I'm spying on Jordan right now, only because he is the only one at the table today. I told Brandy that I can't tell if her messages have come through or not. She decides to call the phone. I see Jordan pull his phone out of his pocket and laugh as he hits the decline button and put it back in his pocket. DAMN!!! I have to tell her.

(Sadie): HEY!! His phone rang. He declined it and put it back in his pocket after he laughed.

"You're not going to answer that call?" I ask Jordan as he puts his phone back in his pocket.

"Nope. It was just some girl that wants to hook up," he says as he smiles.

"Oh, really?" I ask, not believing him.

"Yeah," he smirks.

Brandy: Do you think it is him?
(Sadie): Did Sam answer?
Brady: No
(Sadie): Neither did Jordan.

Brandy

Sam: Hey.
Me: Hey.
Sam: Sorry about not texting today.
Me: Or answering your phone.

Sam: I saw where you called me... not going to get answers that easy, baby.

Me: Baby?

Sam: Yes. You are going to be my girl.

Me: You think so?

Sam: Yes, I do.

Me: Arrogant much?

Sam: LOL, no. Just confident. You're still texting me, so there must be some interest there. I'm sure interested in you and I'm willing to piss off your brother to talk to you. That must mean something, right?

Me: I guess.

Sam: Why did you call me today? Was it to try to find out who I am?

Me: Maybe.

Sam: You'll find out. Two weeks from now at the Halloween party, I want to spend time with you. I'll have a costume on that will cover my face. You won't see my face when I see you in person, but I will see you. I need to see you. See if we have the same chemistry, I think we will.

Me: You think we have chemistry?

Sam: Yes. I feel it every time I'm close to you. I want to see if you feel it, too.

Truth is, just texting him gives me butterflies. I love getting to know him more and I sure hope we have the same feelings when we meet in person.

The next two weeks go by faster than I expected. Sam and I text more and more each passing day.

I still see the three guys at school. None of them act any different around me than they always have. I'm beginning to think that it isn't any of the three of them. At this point, I'm not sure that I care about that. I like talking to him and miss him when I don't hear from him. He tells me I'm his girl and I don't even mind hearing that.

We haven't been able to catch any of them, either. Either it isn't them or he's just too good.

"You ready for Jordan's Halloween party tomorrow?" Sadie asks as she's sitting on my bed.

"I guess." I think I am. I'm going to physically talk to him, see him and maybe even touch him but still not know who he is.

"I'm excited. I hope he tells you who he is," she says as she smiles.

"Me, too."

I'm having trouble going to sleep. I'm sleepy but I can't stop thinking about him.

>*Me: Hey*
>*Sam: ...*

He's answering.

>*Sam: You okay?*
>*Me: I can't sleep.*
>*Sam: You nervous?*
>*Me: Yes.*
>*Sam: Don't be.*
>*Me: Why can't you sleep?*
>*Sam: Who said I was awake?*
>*Me: Oh, shit. I didn't mean to wake you.*
>*Sam: You didn't. I can't sleep, either. LOL!*
>*Me: Ass.*
>*Sam: Yeah, that's why I can't sleep.*

>*Sam: Thinking about your fine ass and how I will have to control myself tomorrow night to not grab it is keeping me up.*
>*Me: LOL!*
>*Sam: You laugh, but I'm serious. I want to kiss you so badly. I can't think of anything else.*
>*Me: Maybe I'll let you kiss me.*
>*Sam: DAMMIT!!!! Now I will never get to sleep.*

Me: Sorry. :(

Sam: I'm not... but I may have something I need to do before I go to bed now.

Me: What's that?

Sam: A cold shower. ;)

Our conversations have been getting more and more flirty. We talk about real things, as much as he will tell me without telling me who he is but then it tends to get flirty. I know what I do to him. He's told me. He's had to "take care of himself" a few times after our conversations. I'm thinking that tonight is going to be another one of those nights.

Me: Do I excite you?

Sam: OMG YES!!! I could send you a picture of what you do to me if it wouldn't scare you away.

Me: You just have those kinds of pictures on your phone?

Sam: No. But I could take one, now, because I am going to be popping the buttons on my pajama pants if you keep talking to me like this.

I can't help but smile. Is it wrong that I enjoy turning him on? I'm excited to "see" him tomorrow now. No more nerves. They're gone.

Me: I'm going to say goodnight now. I'll let you sort yourself out. Lol!

Sam: You laugh now... but you did this to me.

Me: Goodnight.

Sam: Goodnight, my girl.

Yep, there it is. He always says that now at the end of our conversations. I think I like it.

CHAPTER SIX

HALLOWEEN PARTY

The Halloween party is at Jordan's tonight. It's in the field, as usual. Sadie comes over so we can get ready together. Sadie is going to be a vampire. I decided on Red Riding Hood. I remember him saying his favorite color is red, so I play to that. I have on a long red skirt that has a slit up most of my right leg. The top is an off the shoulder white top that has a tight black vest that comes just under my breasts. It's complete with a long, dark red, velvet cape and some black knee-high boots and black gloves. I hope he'll like it.

"Wow, girl. You are hot!" Sadie says as I step out of the bathroom.

"Thanks," I say as I play with the tie of the cape.

"He is for sure going to lose his shit tonight." She laughs.

I'm hoping so. I want him to tell me who he is tonight. I need to know. I want to talk to him tonight. I may actually want to kiss him. Sadie takes my picture and sends it to James. He immediately texts back.

James: Damn, girl. I'm gay and I want to do you.
Me: LOL!

I think he approves. Now, let's hope that Sam does.

We are ready to go to the party. Brian has already left to go pick up Jenny. Jenny has been texting me some, too, asking about Sam. She says she has been trying to get it out of the guys if any of them have been texting me while she is hanging out with them. No luck yet.

Sadie and I head on over to Jordan's. I'm a little nervous. I decide that on the ride over since Sadie is driving, I'll text Sam.

Me: Hey.
Sam: Hey, yourself.
Me: Are you as nervous as I am?
Sam: Maybe even more.
Me: How will I know it's you?
Sam: You won't at first. But before the night is over, I will make sure to spend some time with you... as Sam.
Me: How?
Sam: I will text you and tell you where to go. I will meet you there, in the dark, with a full-face mask on. I already have it ready. The rest of the night, I will just be me.
Me: So, I will be spending the evening around you and not know it's you?
Sam: Yes.
Me: Sam...
Sam: Brandy...
Sam: Soon, baby. I promise.
Me: Okay, I guess.
Sam: That's my girl.
Me: Is it wrong I like it when you call me your girl? And I don't even know who you are yet?

Sam: No. I just hope you want me to keep calling you that when you do know who I am.

Me: Me, too.

Sam: See you soon, baby.

Me: Not if I see you first lol.

Sam: Smartass.

Me: You love my ass.

Sam: I sure do. See you soon!

"What is lover boy saying?" Sadie asks smiling as she is driving. I tell her what all he said. She just smiles bigger. "I think you are going to fall head over heels for this guy."

"I don't know. I guess I'll find out." I'm not sure I want to tell her that I'm already starting to like him. She probably already knows that but I'm not ready to admit it to anyone else. I don't know who he is, and I already can't wait to talk to him daily. I miss him when he's busy and I love it that he wants to see me, touch me, kiss me. Ugh. I want all that, too.

Once we get to the field, I can see all the others in their costumes. Brian and Jenny haven't seen mine yet. I see them over by his truck and Sadie and I walk over to them. Jenny sees me and jumps off and runs over.

"Damn girl, you are hot!" Jenny exclaims.

"Thanks," I say as she's already hugging me. I've always liked her but in the last two weeks, we have become even closer.

"Wow, sis. That is some costume," Brian says as he looks at me. I take a spin.

"You like?" I laugh.

"Not what I was expecting, but it looks good." He smiles at me. He's a good brother.

"Thanks, bro."

"Damn girl... you trying to kill the guys around here?" I hear someone from behind me say. I turn to see David.

"Hi, David," I say as I smile at him. No clue if he is Sam. I sit beside Jenny on the tailgate.

"Hi, Brandy," Jordan says as he looks me up and down. "Sadie." He also looks at her but not in the same way.

"Jordie," I say as I smile at him. James says he thinks it's Jordan.

"Damn that name," he laughs. "I told you, I deserve an upgrade." He laughs again and winks at me. Brian gives him a dirty look and Jordan just laughs harder. "Chill bro," he says to Brian as he takes a seat beside me on the tailgate. "I offered to show her I deserved the upgrade and she turned me down." Brian looks like he could kill him right now. "At least for now." Jordan laughs again.

"That's my sister, dude. Stop being a creep," Brian tells him.

"Look at her. She's hot," Jordan says like he thinks Brian will agree. He won't.

"Dude, shut it," Brian says again. Jordan stops, for now.

"Hi, Brandy." I hear another voice that is familiar.

"Christian," I say as I smile at him.

"You need a dancing partner tonight?" He asks as he smiles at me.

"Maybe."

He smiles at me as he takes a drink from his red plastic cup. The party is a lot of fun. The costumes are pretty good. David is a biker dude. More precise, a dead biker dude with his throat slit and all. Jordan is a businessman, a zombie businessman. Christian is a lumberjack. He is pretty hot all done up in his flannel and ripped jeans. How have I never noticed that before? I have noticed Jordan is gorgeous, but so has every other female in the tri-state area. David is cute but I think his personality gets in his way most of the time. This could be the reason that he is

Sam. He needs me to see the real him, not the him that everyone thinks he is. But Christian. He is rugged, manly, tall, and sexy. I'm not sure how this fact escaped me all these years.

I take a minute to go to the bathroom in the barn when my phone dings with a text.

It's from Sam.

Sam: Damn girl, you are so sexy. I can't stand it any longer.

Shit... I can't see who's typing. Or who isn't?

Me: You like?

Sam: Shit, yes. I LOVE. Can I see you now?

Me: You going to behave yourself?

Sam: I'll try. But you are causing some serious issues.

Me: Sorry.

Sam: No, you aren't.

Me: You're right. I'm not.

Sam: Can I see you now? Please.

Me: Well, since you said please.

Sam: I will say thank you, too.

Me: Where?

Sam: You in the barn?

Me: Yes. How did you know?

Sam: I can't take my eyes off of you.

Sam: Meet me behind the barn, by the woods.

I get nervous now. I don't want to be back by the woods, in the dark.

Sam: What's wrong, baby?

Me: Nothing.

Sam: Yes, it is. You forget how well I know you.

Me: I...

Sam: You don't have to meet me if you don't want to.

Me: I do.

I tell him about what happened at the first party I was at.

Sam: Dammit, Brandy. You never told Brian?
Me: No.
Sam: You don't have to meet me there. We can do it later.

No, I'm not going to let some idiots ruin this. I'm going to meet Sam.

Me: I'm there now.
Sam: You don't have to do this.
Me: I know. I want to.
Sam: Okay. I will be right there. I'm going to come up behind you. Don't be scared.
Me: Okay.

Just a few minutes later I hear someone stepping up behind me. I try not to get scared but those memories from that first night come back to me. At least the few that I remember.

I hear someone whisper to me. I can't tell who it is. "It's okay, baby. It's me... Sam."

"Sam." His name comes out breathy and barely audible.

I close my eyes. I feel him standing behind me. I'm no longer nervous. It's Sam. It's the guy I have been talking to.

"Can I touch you?" he asks, his voice clearer now that he has removed the mask he said he would be wearing. It's still a whisper and I cannot make out his voice. That might be from my own heart beating in my ears.

I want him to touch me. "Yes."

I hear him let out a deep breath as his hands touch my waist from where he is standing behind me. "My God, you feel good." His hands go down my hips and he lightly cups my ass.

I lean back into him. "You are perfect," he says as he moves closer to me. I can feel his body against my back. He moves my hair to one side just like I wore it that day he said he wanted to kiss my neck. "You smell so good." His breath is on my neck. Followed by his lips. I hear him moan as he kisses my neck. "Mm."

His hands are on my stomach and I place mine on top of his. I'm too into the way his mouth feels on my neck to even try to figure out who he is.

"I want to kiss you."

Do I want to kiss him? Yes, I think I do. No, I know I do. It will be my first real kiss. I hope I'm good at it.

"May I kiss you?" he asks.

"Yes." I hear him chuckle at how that small word came out of my mouth. He turns me around to face him slowly. It's too dark to see who he is. I can tell he is taller than I am. I put my hands on his shoulders. He has muscles. I can feel how hard his body is. His hands are on the small of my back as he pulls me closer to him. One hand leaves my back to cup my face. I close my eyes as his lips touch mine. They are so soft. He pulls back a little. "I don't know how I am ever supposed to stop kissing you."

I pull him by the neck down to meet my lips again. That small kiss was not even close to enough. He chuckles as he leans in and presses his lips to mine again. This time his lips move against mine. He pulls me into him, and he slides his hand that was on my back down to my ass. He grabs it and squeezes as he moans into the kiss. I feel his tongue slide across my lips. I open my mouth and let him have access. I feel his tongue slide against mine. It makes me want to massage his, so I do. His kiss is harder, more passionate, his hand pulls me into him. I can feel how excited he's getting. He quickly pulls back from me. I miss his touch. I miss his lips on mine.

"Don't go," I beg. I don't want him to leave me yet.

"I have to," he says with regret in his voice.

"Why?" I instantly fear I did something wrong.

"Because if I don't, I may not stop myself," his voice deep and breathy.

I giggle at his confession.

"I will see you again soon, baby," he says as he pulls out of my arms.

"Sam."

"You're my girl," he says as he steps back from me.

I nod. I can't form any words. It's cold where it was just warm. My lips are tender, and I want him back. But he's already gone. Back to the party. Back to the shadows.

I have to know who he is...

CHAPTER SEVEN

AFTER THE KISS

S am is gone and I miss him even more now. I touch my lips with my fingers, and I can almost feel his lips still on mine. I wait a few minutes before I head back to the party myself. I see Brian and Jenny on the back of his truck. I see Sadie talking to some guy and so is James. One of them is going to be kissing him tonight, the question is which one?

Jordan is talking to a girl but doesn't seem that into it. David is playing a drinking game and Christian is talking to my brother. No clues there. I walk over to sit beside Jenny.

"You okay?" she asks looking concerned.

"Perfect," I answer with a smile across my lips. The same lips where Sam's were only a few minutes ago.

"You look flustered," she says as she smiles at me. It takes her a minute, "Ohhh."

I touch my lips again. She smiles at me. She's caught

on. She leans closer to me to whisper. "Was he that good?" I can only nod. She giggles.

That caught Brian's attention. "What's the big secret you two have been on about for the last two weeks?" he asks. He knows there is something but not what.

We both answer "Nothing" at the same time and then start to giggle. That catches David's attention. "Your make-up is a little smeared there, Brandy," he says as he points to his own mouth.

Oh shit. I didn't think about that. If mine is smeared, then maybe he has some of my lipstick on him. I glance at David, none. Jordan, none. Christian, none. Dammit. Of course, he would think to wipe it off first. I am the inexperienced one and didn't think about it smearing.

Brian looks at my face as I try to wipe it away. "What the fuck?" He sounds angry. "Who the fuck has been making out with my sister?" He hollers. No one answers him. He now looks to me. "Who was it, Brandy?" His eyes hold anger. "Whose ass do I need to kick tonight for putting his hands on my sister?"

I roll my eyes at him. He's gotten more attention now. Jordan has left his girl and come to see.

Jordan smiles as he pokes the bear. "By the look of that smile on her face, it isn't his hands you need to worry about."

Brian looks like a cartoon where his head is going to explode off his body. Jordan is laughing and Jenny is trying to calm him.

"Baby. Calm down," she says as she strokes his hair. If I wasn't before, I am happy for her now. He looks down at her and I can see the love he feels for her. "Don't you want her to have what we have?" He relaxes into her touch.

"But..." he protests.

"No buts baby. She's the same age we are. She's smart. She won't let anyone hurt her."

I hear David cough, "Pussy whipped," cough.

Brian turns to go after David.

"The only reason you aren't pussy whipped is because you can't keep one," Brain yells at him as he lunges at David.

Christian steps in front of David. "He isn't worth it, Bri. He's an ass."

I agree with Christian. I sure hope Sam isn't David. I can't imagine having my first, amazing kiss with such an ass.

Brain sits back on the tailgate of his truck and Jenny is holding his hand. David decides he hasn't had enough apparently. Either he is drunk or just plain stupid. "And how do you know that I wasn't the one that made her smile like that?"

That was all he needed to hear. Brian came off that truck faster than he runs during a game. He tackles David to the ground and throws a punch to his face. He gets in at least two good ones before Christian and Jordan pull him off. David's nose is bleeding, and his lip is busted. He still must run his mouth some more. "Maybe you should ask your sister who it was."

Brian turns to look at me. I can't believe one of the best nights I have ever had is being ruined. Both by my brother and that loudmouth, David. I am secretly praying that David is not Sam because he is acting like such an ass, I could never forgive him for this little display.

Sadie puts her arm around my shoulders and I get off the truck. She takes me to her car, and it is only then that I let the tears fall. I am so upset right now, I just wanted to be happy with being able to kiss Sam. Now the memory is tainted, if not ruined completely.

I sit on Sadie's passenger seat, my feet hanging out the open door and put my head down on my hands. "I'm so sorry," I say between sobs.

"David is an ass and right now, your brother isn't behaving much better." She puts her hand on my back and rubs circles, trying to calm me. I hear a knock on the side of the car. I look up and see Christian standing there.

"Are you okay?"

"Yeah, I will be," I say drying my eyes.

Christian puts his hand out to me and I take it. He helps me stand and he puts his arms around me. I feel comfortable in his arms. I lay my head on his chest and he rubs my back. I notice he is just about the same height as Sam. Nothing else is familiar about him from the kiss but then again, I was so nervous most of the details were a blur. Height isn't going to help me though, because there is less than an inch difference in height between Jordan and Christian.

"Are you sure you're okay?" Christian asks as he kisses the top of my head.

I nod my head against his chest.

"Your brother is just trying to protect you."

"I don't need his protection," I mumble. "I can take care of myself."

"I'm sure you can. We guys don't have a great track record with girls, and he knows it," he hesitates. "He doesn't want to see you hurt."

I pull back and look up at him. He's cute when he smiles at me. "It's just..." I don't know if I can tell him.

"Just what?"

I take a deep breath. I have to tell someone. Sadie has excused herself back to the party. "It's just," I hesitate again. He looks at me and smiles. "I was having the best night ever before all that drama."

"Oh, really?" he chuckles. "Would that have to do with why your makeup was smeared?"

My face gets hot and red. "Yes." I nod.

I see a flicker of something come across his face and then it's gone. Was that jealousy I saw? "Well, he is a very lucky guy."

"After tonight, I'm sure he won't ever speak to me again," I sigh as another tear falls.

"He most certainly will. But, if for some reason he doesn't, he isn't worth your time."

"You think?" I ask almost too excitedly. He chuckles.

"I know."

He hugs me again before he takes a small step back. "You ready to go back to the party?" he asks as he loosens his grip on me.

"Yeah. Will you go with me?"

I see him smirk as he puts his arm around my shoulder. "Of course."

We walk back to the party with Christian's arm over my shoulders. He pulls me close to his body again as we walk. We get to the truck and Brian looks at us. He sees Christian's arm over my shoulders and gives him a dirty look. I stare back at him. "Don't say one fucking word. If you hadn't acted like as big of an ass as David did, I wouldn't need someone to look after me." I glare at him. "So, before you want to kick Christian's ass, just know you are the reason he felt like he had to comfort me."

Brian looks down at his hands. "I'm sorry, Brandy." Jenny takes his hand in hers. "It's just that David is an ass. He is a skank. He uses girls for one thing and as soon as he gets it, he leaves them. I don't want that for you."

"I don't, either, but don't you think I am smart enough to figure that out?"

He looks like a scolded child. "Yes." He gets down and

comes over to me and hugs me. That's the only time Christian has let go of me since he came to the car. "I'm sorry."

I hug him back. "I forgive you. Just don't do it again. I'm a big girl, ya know?"

"I know," he says as he lets go of me. He looks at Christian. "Thank you for looking out for her. Sorry I was an ass."

"No problem. Jordan had you, so I went to her. No big deal," Christian says as he steps back a little. He is still near me but not touching me anymore.

I go to get a drink and I hear someone behind me. "Hey, you okay?" I look up to see Jordan.

"Yeah, thanks," I say as I take a drink.

"I wanted to tell you earlier how good you look but you kind of disappeared," he smiles at me like he knows something.

"Yeah, I..."

"No need to explain. That huge smile on your face and smeared makeup tells me all I need to know," he smirks again.

I roll my eyes at him before I smile at him. He is sweet, even when he's a butt.

He leans in to whisper to me. "I'm glad to see that smile back on your face. You are way too pretty to frown." He kisses my cheek and then turns and walks away. I go back to where Sadie is and sit beside her.

"What the hell happened?"

I tell her about the meeting, the kiss, how great it was and then about how David mentioned my make up being smeared, which set off my brother. Then I tell her about how Christian held me and kissed my head and then Jordan told me how pretty I was tonight and kissed my cheek. James came over during the conversation and listened to the end. I repeated what he missed.

"Damn, I missed a lot," he smiles.

"Where were you?" we both ask him.

"Uh," he smiles. Okay, questions answered. It would be James that would be kissing the boy they were both talking to earlier. Damn, that boy is a dog.

We all laugh. The three of us hang out for the rest of the evening. I see Brian watching me, trying to figure out who I was kissing. I want to tell him to join the club. We are all trying to figure it out. But I think that may not make the situation better. I see both Jordan and Christian watching me. I even saw David look my way a few times after he got his bleeding to stop. My phone vibrates in my pocket. I take it out and see a message from Sam.

Sam: Hey, baby. Are you okay?

Me: Yes. Are you?

Sam: Yeah. I'm good. I wasn't the one that got hit tonight.

I take a deep breath and I'm relieved. It's not David, because he sure as shit got hit tonight.

Sam: But, if I did it would have been worth it. That kiss was amazing. I can't help but want to do it again. Ass whipping be damned.

Me: I want to do it again, too.

"What is he saying?" Sadie asks as she is trying to read over my shoulder. James is trying on the other side. "Oh, thank goodness, it isn't David. He's an ass." We all three laugh.

Sam: What are you laughing about?

Me: You're still here?

Sam: Yes, I will be here all night.

I can't stop smiling thinking of him being here all night. And how he wanted to hold me and kiss me the last time he was here.

Me: Me, too.

Sam: Damn. Now I want to kiss you again.

Me: You know where I am.

"Damn, Brandy. You are getting brave." James laughs.

"You would, too, for another kiss like that." My face gets hot. I want to kiss him again.

Sam: You're blushing.

Me: Thinking of our kiss.

Sam: You staying in the same stall again?

Me: Yes.

Sam: Maybe I will come and kiss you again.

I look up and smile. I can't see him, but I know he can see me. I just nod my head.

Sam: I saw that. When your friend has gone to sleep and it's dark, I will sneak in and I'll kiss you again. As long as you promise not to kick my ass like Brian did to David. ;)

Me: I promise.

Sam: See you soon, baby.

CHAPTER EIGHT

THE REVEAL

S*am*

Tonight was the best night I have ever had. I'm not a virgin, by no means but Brandy is. I told her I know that she has never had a real boyfriend. I was trying to tell her I knew, without saying *I know you're a virgin*. I don't care that she is. I've liked her for years, but her brother is one of my best friends. He is the type of friend that will be my friend even when we are old and married with grandkids.

I've wanted to talk to her for years, but I was afraid to tell her and ruin my friendship with Brian. You may be wondering why I'm willing to risk it now. The last party in the field, after homecoming, I wanted to tell her. I know she heard the conversation me and the other two guys had in the barn that night. We weren't exactly quiet with our conversation about her. I didn't know she was in there at the time but later, I came back to check and make sure everyone was okay, I saw her and Sadie cuddled in one of the stalls. She was so peaceful as she slept. I just wanted to hold her.

I had already texted her and she was convinced that I had the wrong number. I didn't have her number before and I knew she didn't have mine, but I got hers from Brian's phone. I knew who I was texting. I stood and watched her sleep for a few minutes before I slept in the stall across from her. I wanted to make sure she was okay. I had wondered if she was the girl that I had heard was attacked freshman year at the first party of the year. I was afraid to ask her or Brian back then and she never came to another one, until that first night. If it was her, I was going to make sure to protect her.

I've never been in love before. I have never pretended to be and have never said it to any person other than my parents. But Brandy is the type of girl I could fall in love with. She is the type of girl that's an end game. The one you marry and commit your entire life to. She deserves that and I wanted to give it to her. Hearing David talk about her that night pissed us both off. He would just want to fuck her, and he'd leave her after that. That was what he did. I wasn't much better, but I never lied to a girl to get them to fuck me. They all knew the score. They knew I was not in love, not going to fall in love and wasn't going to put a ring on it.

The next morning, I woke before her and Sadie. I watched her again. She was safe and it was light out. I sent her another text. I was in it now. I made the decision to go for it. I was for sure not going to let David try anything with her. Shit, I would kick his ass myself before Brian even knew he had tried.

I was nervous to tell her I liked her. I have never been nervous with a girl before. Being popular and a football player made it easy to get girls. But not the one I want. The one I have wanted for years. She can move that sexy body of hers. She danced with her friend and that got the attention of many of the guys at the party. Yeah, I wasn't going to lose my chance to be one of them. I could see that David was eyeing her and that fucker was NOT going to move in on her.

We've been texting since that day. We've gotten flirty and I love it. Almost every time I talk to her, I have had to, uh... sort myself out-as she calls it. I call it being a horny teenage guy flirting with the one girl he wants all the damn time. We've gotten more and more brave over text. I just have to touch her. I have to feel her lips on mine. Her soft body in my arms. I can't stand it any longer.

I tell her about my idea for the Halloween party. I'm not sure if I can tell her who I am yet, but I can't stand not kissing her. I was shocked and so happy when she agreed. But then she confirmed it was her that night so many years ago. I never thought meeting there would be an issue for her. I guess I hoped it wasn't her.

She was tough, though. She met me there and I could touch her. I kissed her lips and she pulled me back for more. I had to finally break the kiss because if I didn't, I was going to take it too far. Further than I wanted to take it in the field with all the team around and being intoxicated. If she is a virgin like I think she is, she deserves better than that for her first time. Don't get me wrong, I wanted to. I want to right now, but I won't. She deserves better and I will give it to her. I want to be her first and I'm afraid that I may just want to be her last, too.

David, being the usual ass that he is, starts something with Brian. He comments her makeup is smeared. Yeah, I did that. I smeared it when I kissed the hell out of her. And now, dammit, I want to do it again. We pull Brian off of David and calm him and Brandy down. One of us takes Brian and one of us takes Brandy. (You didn't think I was going to tell you before I tell Brandy who I am, did you?)

I go into the stall where I am planning on sleeping. Across from hers again. They're talking and they didn't hear me slide in there. I can be sneaky when I need to be and right now, I need to be.

There is no more noise from their stall. It sounds like they're asleep now. I send her a text so that she won't be scared if she is still awake.

Me (Sam): I'm coming in now, baby.

I get no response, so I decide to go on in and see her. She knows I am. I promised I would. I always keep my promises and it is even more important to keep all of my promises to her.

I am standing outside of the stall where I can see them sleeping. It is now or never. I turn my cell on so I can have a little bit of light. I step into the stall and run my hand over her face. She stirs and I smile at her. She can't see my face yet, but it won't be long before she does.

"Sam?" she asks in a sleepy whisper.

"Yes, baby, it's me," I say as I take her hand in mine. "Come with me."

I use my cell phone to light our path out of the stall. The light is facing away from us so she still can't see my face. I love how she trusts me. I would never hurt her. I want to protect her. I would beat anyone that tried to hurt her. If I knew who those fuckers were that hurt her back then, I would kick their asses for sure. Her hand feels so good in mine. I hear her yawn as she follows me. I take her to the stall I was planning on sleeping in and quietly close the stall door. I stop and turn her to face me, still in complete darkness.

"I want you to be mine," I whisper in her ear as she melts into my body.

"I am yours," she says as she wraps her arms around my waist and buries her head in my chest. This is not the first time I have ever held her like this, and this time is by far better. Even though I'm holding her as Sam, I am holding her as the person she wants to hold her. The guy talking to her for the last few weeks. The one that talks to her first thing in the morning and before she goes to sleep at night. The man that kissed her earlier tonight and plans on kissing her again, right now.

"I'm going to kiss you," I tell her as I hold her face in my hands. I press my lips to hers. They are just as sweet as they were earlier in the night. But this time, this time I am going to tell her who I am. I can't do this anymore. I need to know if she could ever feel the same way about me. The real me. Flaws and all. She kisses me back with just as much energy and desire as I have for her. Her hands are on my waist and my hands have migrated to her ass. That soft and curvy ass. My God, I just want to squeeze it every time I see her. I know she feels like she isn't worthy of love or attention from a guy. She feels unattractive and that is so far from the truth. She is the most attractive girl I have ever met. All that she thinks is unattractive about herself is what I like. I love her curves. I prefer a woman with some curves to them. What's that old saying? *More cushion for the pushin'.* Yeah, I am on board with that. Damn, I have to stop thinking like that while I'm kissing her. She's going to feel what she's doing to my body and I don't want her to think it's all about sex for me. Yes, I want to have sex with her, but only when she's ready.

She moans into the kiss and that does it. Full steam ahead. I now have a full mast. For those that don't speak code... I have a massive hard-on. And not just massive because it's massive... even though it is... but because she makes me harder than I have ever been before. A small breath from her on my skin would send me over the edge.

I kiss on her neck as she lets out a small moan. I need to stop this before we wake up everyone else in here. Not to mention I want to take it so much further.

"Baby," I whisper to her as I pull back.

"Don't go," she pleads.

I chuckle. "I'm not leaving. I'd very much like for you to stay in here with me tonight."

I can hear her take a breath in. I'm not sure what she thinks I'm asking for. "Not sex, baby. Just more kissing and to hold you tonight."

I hear her let out the breath and her body relaxes into mine again.

Brandy
He just asked me to stay with him. I instantly cringed. He must have felt it because he said not for sex. Just to hold me and kiss me more. I want that, too.

"Are you going to tell me who you are first?"

I feel him tense now. I want to tell him I already like him and that isn't going to change since I already know he isn't David.

"Do you want me to?" he asks.

"Yes."

I hear and feel him take a deep breath and he turns his phone around so that some light is on his face. I close my eyes before the light hits his face, as I try to prepare to see him.

"You can look, baby," he says as he chuckles. "It's time."

He kisses my lips one more time and I slowly open my

eyes. It takes just a second to adjust to the light and for my brain to register who it is. I get a huge smile on my face as I touch his cheek with my hand. He leans into me and closes his eyes.

"Christian?"

$$\overline{\hspace{3cm}}$$

CHAPTER NINE

$$\overline{\hspace{3cm}}$$

OUR NIGHT TOGETHER

He opens his eyes and looks at me. It looks like he is waiting for me to realize I don't want it to be him and turn and leave. That couldn't be further from the truth.

"Yes, baby. It's me," he places his hand over mine that's on his face. "Are you disappointed?"

I vigorously shake my head no. He chuckles. "No?" he asks as a small smile spreads across his lips.

"No." I smile at him, "I'm glad it's you. I wanted it to be you."

His hands are on both of my cheeks, holding my face to look at him. He licks his lips just before he kisses me again. This time I grab his neck and pull him into me even harder. It's Christian. He is Sam. My Sam. My Christian. He grabs a hold of me as he lowers my body to the floor. His body hovering over mine as he continues to kiss me. His kiss is hungry. His body is tense, still hovering over mine. I wrap my arms around his back and pull him down. His body is now resting on mine. I can feel how very excited this is making him. It's doing the same thing to me. His kiss moves to my neck as he lightly bites and sucks. Just as quickly he stops and rolls to the side. I am cold once again. Every time he leaves me, I get cold. I miss him.

"What's wrong?" I ask as I touch his face with my hands. My Christian.

"We have to stop."

"Okay?" I say, trying not to sound disappointed.

He chuckles again.

"Not here. Not like this. We have been drinking and I don't want to..." he pauses.

"You know, don't you?" I ask trying to will him to just say it.

He sighs. "Yes."

"Shit." I start to pull away from him.

"No. Don't go, please," he says as he tightens his grip on me.

"I'm so embarrassed."

"Don't be." He leans in and kisses my lips quickly. "It's one of the best things about you."

I laugh. "We are talking about me being a virgin, right?"

"Yes. We are. And I love it that no one else has ever been able to make you feel the things that I will."

I take in a deep breath. Did he just say that he will?

"Yes, that is what I said," he laughs. "I want to be your first but not here. Not like this. And only when you're ready."

"What if I'm ready now?" I say as I nuzzle into him more.

"You really are perfect, aren't you?"

He presses his hips into me. I can feel him. He is for

sure ready. "I want it to be special. Something we will cherish forever. Not some half-drunken night in a barn full of teens that could hear us. I don't want just one time with you, Brandy. I want something real. I want us... well, to be an us."

"I do, too," I say as I nuzzle into his chest. He wraps his arms around me and I feel good. I feel like I'm where I'm supposed to be. He leans in and kisses me again. This time when he pulls back, he buries his face in my hair and tightens his grip on me.

We end up making out for a little while. I get brave and suck on his neck. I know what it does to him when he buries his head in my neck to keep from making too much noise. He pulls back and wraps his arms around me, holding me close to him.

"I have set my alarm to be up before the sun comes up. That way you can go back to Sadie and I can hold you the rest of the night."

I nod. I cuddle into his chest and listen to his breathing. He pulls the blanket up around us and we fall asleep in each other's arms.

The next morning, I am woken by sweet kisses to my neck and cheeks.

"Good morning, beautiful," he says as he pulls me closer to him.

"Morning," I say as I snuggle into him.

"It will be light out soon. You should go back across the aisle, so no one sees you in here."

I know that I should, but I don't want to. I don't know what this means for us. I know who he is now, and I'm happier than I could have imagined. I spent my first night with a guy and I would say it was innocent. At least compared to what it could have been. I'm happy it's him. Now I know why I felt so calm after all the drama with

Brian and David when I was in his arms. My brother even thanked him for comforting me. Maybe he would be okay with us together. I guess we'll find out.

"I know, I just don't want to leave your arms. I just found out who you are, and I'm not ready to go back to just texting yet."

He laughs. "Oh, we are not going back to just texting, baby. Not after last night. But I'm not sure after last night your brother is exactly ready to accept this."

"So, what are we going to do?" I ask as I kiss on his neck.

"Fuck. I know what I want to do if you keep doing that," he laughs as I kiss his neck again, biting and then sucking on the same spot from last night. He bites his lip to keep from making any noise. I notice that I left a big mark. Good, even if I can't tell anyone yet it's me, I want other girls to know he is taken.

He laughs, "Did you just mark me?"

I smile, "Maybe."

"I have totally changed my mind, you are such a bad girl." His lips are on mine again. "And I love it."

I know I need to go but I don't want to. I lean in and kiss him one more time before I stand to leave. He stands with me. "I'm going to miss you," I tell him as he wraps his arms around me.

"I'll see you soon, I promise," he says as he kisses me one last time before I leave the privacy of our spot. I sneak in beside Sadie and she never even moves. My phone lights up and I see a text.

> *Sam: I miss you already.*
> *Me: I can come back. ;)*
> *Sam: If you do, you aren't leaving again.*
> *Me: Deal.*
> *Sam: Anytime you are ready, baby. I'm here.*

Me: I don't want us to keep this secret forever.

Sam: We won't, I promise. I can't wait to kiss those lips anytime I want, no matter who sees.

Me: Me, too.

Sam: Get some more sleep, baby.

Me: You, too.

I drift off to sleep with a huge smile on my face. I get another two hours of sleep before I wake up again. I don't hear any noises in the barn. I wonder if Christian is still over there sleeping. I want to go check but if I do and get caught, it's too risky.

I decided to leave his name as Sam in my phone. I didn't want anyone to see it and know that I have been texting him. Just a little while longer. After the blow-up last night, we have to wait a little bit longer. My brother had a fit when I was just caught kissing someone. How will he feel when he finds out it's Christian?

I smell food cooking. The day after many of Jordan's parties there is food. They cook a couple of pots of Mountain Man breakfasts and a few other things. It's always so good. I can smell it cooking already. I shake Sadie.

"Food is cooking," I say as she opens her eyes and takes a deep breath.

"Yummy."

I want to tell her I met him last night and I know who he is, but I'm not ready just yet.

We get up and clean ourselves off. I'm glad we brought sweat clothes to sleep in last night. We put our blankets away and we can hear the boys talking by the fire.

"Dammit Christian. What type of vampire got a hold of your neck last night?" Jordan teases.

I hear Christian laugh, "I don't know what you're talking about."

I peek around the corner and see Jordan looking at

Christian's neck. I know what he is looking at. He's looking at the very same place that I marked him last night. I didn't mean to do it but afterwards I was glad that I did.

"Damn. That's a helluva mark," Brian says as he's looking at Christian's neck, too.

"What's going on out there?" Sadie asks.

"Let's go find out," I say, knowing exactly what's going on.

We walk out and see the guys all standing by the fire. I see Christian look up when I walk outside, and I see the small smile he gives me. I blush right away. I know what they were just talking about and I also know I am the one that put it there.

"Holy shit Christian," Sadie pipes in. She is staring at the mark on his neck. I notice it for the first time in the light and I can't help but smile. Leave it to Sadie to not let something go, "What the hell happened to you? I'm surprised with a mark like that you didn't wake up the whole barn."

I can't help it, I laugh.

She goes at it again, "If it wasn't good enough to make you scream out, it should have at least hurt enough to get some noise out of you." She walks over and touches his neck. "Damn, I bet that shit hurt. You must have been getting it good to let someone mark you like that."

I laugh again. I remember him having to bite his lip and bury his face to keep from making any noise when I did it.

"You guys slept across from him," Jordan says as he looks at me and Sadie. "Didn't you guys hear anything?"

I shrug my shoulders, "I guess maybe he's just quiet."

Jordan and Brian laugh. Christian just smiles. I feel my face flush. I have to get that under control before someone sees me and puts it together.

"Who is she, Chris?" my brother asks.

Jordan throws in, "And are you seeing her again? If not, can you pass her number to me?" He laughs. "I wouldn't mind spending some time with any girl that can suck like that."

"No, I will not pass her number along to you, and yes, I will see her again, just as soon as I can," he smiles as I catch him looking at me. I can't wait to see him again.

"Damn, that must have been some good shit," Brain teases him. "Did you see that, Jenny?"

Jenny just laughs. "Yes, everyone in a mile radius can see it."

Christian blushes. I have never seen him blush before. "Can we maybe not talk anymore about my girl?" My heart skips a beat hearing him call me his girl in front of everyone. Even if they don't know it's me that he's talking about.

"Your girl?" Brian asks.

"When did you get a fucking girl? Was she at the party last night? FUCK!! Why do you always get the good ones?" Jordan says, acting jealous.

I can't lie. I don't like hearing about him getting the 'good ones'. It makes me jealous.

"Well, she is my girl. And no other girl could even come close to comparing to her." That makes me feel a little better. I know he has a past, and I know he's not a virgin, but I also know he has not been with anyone else since we started talking. We did talk about that last night. I'm happy about that.

A few of the other girls come out that stayed last night. All the guys are looking at them, trying to figure out if they did this to him. One of the few girls that he has ever been seen with was this girl named Brittany. She's a cheerleader and dated around just as much as the guys did. He had been seen with her a few times, but it was never anything serious that I could tell. I see her walk up to him and the guys are eyeing her. I know he didn't spend the night with her, but they don't.

"Did you do that to our boy, Brittany?" Jordan asks.

"Do what?" she looks at Christian's neck where Jordan is pointing.

She laughs, "Nope. Wasn't me. I was... busy... last night."

Yeah, she hooked up with someone else. Good. Stay away from my man.

"Okay, yes, I have a huge ass hickey on my neck. Last night was the best night of my life. Now, can we eat and stop talking about my girl?"

Brittany looks right at him. "Your girl?"

CHAPTER TEN

AFTER OUR FIRST NIGHT

I don't know how this is going to go but no one was expecting him to claim someone as his girl. She doesn't look impressed.

He just looks right at her, "Yes, my girl." He smirks as if he is proud to say, 'his girl'. "I have a girl and yes, she is the one that did this to me last night. She was at the party and last night was better than I could have even imagined. And to answer your question again, Jordan. Yes, I will be seeing her again. As often as she will see me, and I will not be seeing anyone else. So, now can we eat and stop talking about me and my girl and what we did or didn't do last night?"

"Shit," Jordan says, stunned. "How drunk was I last night that I missed Christian fucking some girl?"

Christian rolls his eyes and just tries to ignore Jordan's comment.

"I can't believe Christian has a girl," Sadic says as we

get a plate to get our food. "I guess that answers if he is Sam or not, huh?"

Yeah, it does. But she doesn't know it yet. I can't tell her right now. There are too many people here to risk saying it. I will tell her later.

I just nod. I see him talking to my brother and Jordan. I see him looking at me and when I catch him, he just smiles.

"Have you heard from Sam today?" she asks as she takes a bite.

"Yes, I talked to him this morning," I say following behind her in taking a bite.

"What did he say?"

We continue eating and talking, "He wants to see me again, soon."

She gets excited. If she only knew I spent most of the night in his arms last night.

"So, if it isn't David and Christian obviously hooked up last night, it must be Jordan, right?"

I can't take it anymore; I have to tell her. I lean over to whisper to her. "If I tell you something, you have to promise to keep it a secret. Swear. You can't react, not here."

She nods.

"I spent the night with Sam last night," I say as she squeals. All the guys look over at us, especially Christian. He smirks. He knows I'm telling her who he is. He just smiles at me.

"You did what?" she says, much lower.

I explain about the messages, how he came to get me in the dark, how he kissed me and finally... I tell her who he is.

"WHAT?!?!" she yells.

"Damn, girls. What the hell is so interesting?" Jordan asks.

We both laugh. Sadie speaks up, "Did you know that *Days of Our Lives* was renewed for another season?" The guys just shake their heads and Christian laughs. Yeah, he knows.

It takes her a second, but I see it on her face... "Oh my God... that hickey... that was you?"

I nod.

"Did you? You know?" she wiggles her eyebrows.

I shake my head, no. She smiles at me and looks over to Christian. I smack her arm and get her attention.

"You can't tell anyone yet. Not until we figure out how to tell my brother," I say as I look at Brian.

She nods. "Damn girl. He's telling everyone you are his."

I smile and nod. I like it. I like it that he's telling everyone that he's taken. They will know by who soon enough.

"It's been him this whole time?" she asks remembering back to the first night. "I guess that dancing with him did something to him." We both laugh.

"I'm going to run to the bathroom," I say as I get up off the log by the fire.

She just nods and smiles.

I go to the bathroom, do my thing and as I'm washing my hands, I hear a knock on the door.

"Someone's in here," I yell out to whomever it is.

I hear his voice, "I know. Let me in."

I unlock the door and open it to see Christian. He smiles as he walks into the bathroom and locks the door behind him.

"What?" is all I managed to get out before his lips are on mine. His hands are on my ass and he lifts me up and sets me on the countertop. He stands between my legs as he kisses me, hard and desperate. "Chris..."

He laughs against my lips. "I had to kiss you again."

I wrap my arms around his neck and pull him to me to kiss me again. "Don't stop."

He pulls my hips closer to the edge of the counter and he steps up closer to me. I can feel him between my legs as I wrap them around behind him. He growls into the kiss.

"I can't take much more of this today," he says as he kisses on my neck. "Maybe I should mark you. So there is no question you belong to me."

I like this side of him. I like it when he is protective and a little possessive. "You're mine."

"I'm yours," I repeat. It's true. I am his. I have no interest in being with any other man.

"I don't like it when Jordan talks about you like that," he says, resting his forehead against mine.

"He's an ass."

We both laugh.

"He is, but I still don't like it."

I sigh. "He wasn't talking about me. He was talking about the girl that gave you this." I run my hand over his mark.

"Well, that is you."

"He doesn't know it though."

He pulls me to him and hugs me. "I am in so much trouble with you."

I pull back from him. I don't know what he means.

He chuckles, "I'm not going to be able to keep my hands to myself around you. Not now. Not since I know what it's like to kiss these lips, to hear you moan with my touch. Dammit, girl. I don't know how to control myself with you."

"Who says you have to?" I smile at him. "We can go

out there and tell them all, right now. Tell them that you're mine and I'm yours."

"Hmmm," he smiles. "Can we?"

"Sure."

He sighs, "And tell your brother, who thinks I fucked some girl last night, that you are the one that did this to me?"

Ugh. Okay, maybe not today.

"How long will it take for that to go away?"

He laughs, "I don't know, are you planning on putting anymore there?"

I kiss on his neck, "Maybe."

"Okay, but just so you know. Next one you put on me, I get to return the favor." He wiggles his eyebrows.

I pull down my shirt so that he can see the area just above my bra. I smirk at him, "Here ya go big boy, have at it."

He chuckles as he kisses on my neck, his lips trailing down to the area that I just exposed. He licks the area and then kisses it. His kiss gets stronger as he starts to suck on my skin. I actually like the sensation of him marking me. I run my fingers through his hair as he continues to kiss and suck on the newly exposed skin.

There's a knock on the bathroom door. I jump back and manage to get out, "I'm coming."

Christian laughs under his breath at my choice of words. I smack his arm. "Not yet, but give me a few minutes," he whispers.

"It's just me," Sadie says through the door. "The guys are looking for Christian."

"Thanks, Sadie," Christian answers. I giggle at him answering her. No use in hiding it from her, she already knows.

Christian lets me off the counter, he adjusts himself in

his jeans and unlocks the door. Sadie opens it, "Sorry to interrupt but they have started to notice that he's missing."

"Thanks," he says to her again. He comes over and leans down and kisses me again. "See you soon, baby." I just nod.

Christian walks out of the bathroom and I splash cold water on my face.

"Damn that was hot," she laughs. "What was going on in here?"

I pull my shirt down and show her the mark that he just made.

"Damn girl."

I dry my hands as she washes hers. We leave the barn together.

"Where did you two go? You just disappeared?" my brother asks.

I look at Christian. He smiles to let me know everything is okay.

"Earth to Brandy. You and Sadie left, you okay?" he asks me again.

"Oh, yeah. You know us girls have to go to the bathroom together," I answer.

Jenny adds in, "True. That is a real thing." I think she just figured it out, too, because she looks between Christian and myself and smiles.

We spend about another hour of eating, laughing and just hanging out. My phone vibrates in my pocket and I take it out. I see a text from Sam.

Sam: Is it bad I can't stop thinking about kissing you and how I want to see if all of you is as sweet as what I have tasted so far?

Me: Only if it is wrong that I want you to do it, as well.

Sam: Damn, bathroom again?

I laugh out loud. My brother looks at me. I see Jenny

looking at me, I know she knows I'm texting Sam. I'm not sure she knows who he is for sure, yet.

I look over and see Christian adjusting himself again. I just smirk at him. He shrugs his shoulders at me.

Me: You okay?

Sam: No.

Me: Anything I can do?

I see him get a huge smile on his face.

Sam: Stop looking so damn gorgeous?

Me: LOL!

Sam: We are going to have to tell them soon. I am having a hard time not holding you right now. I almost just walked over to you and kissed you when you laughed.

Me: Then do it.

Sam: Really?

I shrug my shoulders at him.

Me: If you want to, yes.

Sam: What if your brother hates me?

Me: He won't. If he does, he will get over it.

Sam: Soon.

Me: Okay.

We put our phones away for now. We just enjoy joking and kidding with our friends. I know that I will have to tell my brother soon that I'm seeing someone. Then I'll have to tell him who that person is. I'm not sure which part worries me the most.

Sam: How about a date tonight? Go to the drive-in with me?

Me: A date? A real date?

Sam: Yes. I will pick you up, take you in my truck, and kiss your beautiful lips goodnight when I bring you home.

Me: What if Brian sees us?

Sam: He is going out with Jenny tonight.

Me: Okay, it's a date.

I see him smiling at his phone. There's a drive-in

nearby. I love going there and it's kind of private since you don't get out of your car. And Christian's truck has dark windows. No one can see through them, especially in the dark at a movie.

I can't stop smiling at my phone. Jordan comes over beside me. "What has that huge smile on your face today, my dear?" I startle at his voice. I didn't hear him come up.

"Oh, nothing. Just making plans for tonight," I answer, hiding my phone.

"Hmmm, Christian has a girl. Your brother beats the hell out of David for pointing out that your lipstick was all smudged from a heavy make out session. I'm wondering if these two things are a coincidence or not?"

"What are you trying to say, Jordie?"

He laughs, "That the two might be related, that's all," he leans in a little closer. "And to tell you that was a hell of a mark that you left on his neck last night." I blush. He smiles, "Ahh, so not such a coincidence."

"Jordie," I say, begging with my eyes not to tell.

"Don't worry. I'm not going to tell anyone. Just don't let it go on too long before you tell Brian. He'll be mad, but he'll get over it. Probably the quicker you tell him the better. He isn't big on secrets. He'll be more upset for you to keep it from him than of you dating Christian."

"It just happened last night," I whisper.

"You mean sex?" he asks smiling.

I shake my head no.

"Ahh, damn, he does like you. You wouldn't be the one he has been texting the last two weeks, would you?"

My face turns red again.

"You are. Okay, so it is you. Don't hurt my boy. He has it pretty bad for you. He hasn't shut up about you for the last two weeks."

"Really?" I ask wanting to know more.

"Yeah. I'm glad he finally decided to tell you who he is. And I'm happy that it's you he was texting. He's liked you for years now."

What? Christian has liked me for years? How did I not know this?

"What?"

Jordan smiles, "Yea, he's talked about this girl that he's had the major hots for going on about three years now. He said he finally texted her and that you have been talking a lot and he wanted to tell you who he was. I've known he's liked you for years and I was hoping it was you he had finally texted, but Brian doesn't know it's you. He knows about the texts though. Not the details or anything. Those were only for his eyes."

"Thanks, Jordan." I smile at him, using his full name.

"I guess I finally got that upgrade, huh?" he punches my arm, gently.

"Yeah, I guess you did."

CHAPTER ELEVEN

FIRST DATES ARE GOOD

It wasn't long after my conversation with Jordan that Sadie took me home. I needed to do a few things and get ready for my date with Christian tonight. I can't believe we are going on an actual date.

I'm ready to go as I wait for him to get to my house. Brian has already left to pick up Jenny. I hear a knock at the door. I answer it and find a handsome Christian standing there. He hands me a single red rose and my face turns almost the same color.

"Hi, beautiful," he says as I walk out the door.

I lean in and kiss him on the cheek. "Thank you."

He opens the door for me and helps me into his truck. After he closes it, he runs around to get in the driver's side. Who knew that he was so sweet?

As we drive to the movie, he holds my hand. It feels good to show affection and not have to worry about who sees us.

He pays for us to get in and we drive in and find a good spot. One that doesn't have too many people on our row, close to the back and the snack stand.

"Is this okay?" he asks as he parks.

"Yeah, it's perfect."

He smiles at me. "Do you want something to snack on? I stopped and got your favorite pizza already and I also got us some drinks in the cooler in the backseat."

I look back and see my favorite pizza and the cooler. He does know me. I guess it helps we have grown up together.

The front of his truck has two seats with part of the middle one that folds down. He reaches down and puts that up and pats the seat beside him. "Come here."

I scoot over so that I am sitting next to him. He puts his arm around me and smiles. "Four whole hours of being able to kiss and touch you as much as I want." The drive-in is always a double feature. We have two scary ones playing tonight on our screen. Even the movie choice he knows I will like.

The movie has started and a scary part is building up. I know it is going to be bad. You can tell by the music that's playing. I bury my head into his chest. He chuckles as he holds me tighter to him. "Come here, babe." He kisses me on the top of my head. I look up to see him watching me. He smiles as he leans down and presses his lips against mine. This was our first official kiss this evening and I am hoping it will not be our last.

After a few minutes of kissing his talented and sweet lips, he pulls back. "I think I would just like to have the rest of the four hours be just like that."

I giggle. So would I.

We do end up watching most of the first movie. But there has been a lot of kissing. We ate our pizza soon after we arrived at the drive-in and so far, it has been the perfect night. I need to go to the bathroom before the next movie starts. He says he will go, too, and we will meet back here. We both get out and I go into one of the bathroom stalls. I hear two girls come in and I can tell that one of them is Brittany. I hear her talking to one of her friends. Oh, great. Just what I need tonight. To run into the one person that would love to tell everyone I am here with Christian.

"Yeah, he said he has a girl. Can you believe that shit?" It sounds like she is talking about Christian.

The other girl responds but I don't recognize her voice. "Maybe you were mistaken. If anyone would be his girl, that should be you."

"I know, right?" she pauses. "I have been putting in the work for a long time for him and this is what he does?"

"Maybe you should have slept with him?" the other girl says. I smile to myself thinking about her not sleeping with him.

"I have tried but he said no. I was beginning to wonder if he was gay. I mean, who turns me down?" Brittany asks as she laughs.

The other girl just states, "Christian."

I can't believe what I'm hearing. Am I hearing correctly that Christian has never slept with Brittany? I know he isn't a virgin, but it makes me happy to know he hasn't been with her like everyone thinks he has. Maybe he isn't as experienced as I thought.

They use the bathroom and leave, still talking about Christian and how sexy he's looking tonight. The other girl tells Brittany that maybe he is on a date tonight, with his girl. This could be trouble.

I wash my hands and make sure to look before I go back to his truck. I hurry up and sneak inside. I'm sure no one saw me. I look in the mirror and I can see Brittany talking to Christian. Now I know why she didn't see me. She was too busy watching for him. I see her try to touch his arm and it hurts my feelings. He steps back and doesn't allow her to put her hands on him. That makes me smile. A minute later I hear his door open and he gets in the truck. I'm still on my side of the truck. He looks at me so far away. He can see on my face that I am upset.

"I assume you saw Brittany?"

"Yes," I answer and don't say anything else.

He pats the seat beside him. I'm hesitant.

"Baby?" he says with a sad look on his face.

I scoot over closer to him. His arm goes around me and the other hand cups my face. "Look at me."

I look in his direction but close my eyes.

"Baby?" he repeats.

I open my eyes and look at him. I see the concern on his face.

"I can't do this," he says as he looks down.

My heart drops. I can only imagine what he is going to say to me. Are we done before we ever get started?

"Can't do what?"

"See you like this. I can't keep us a secret. I almost told her just so she would shut up about us."

"Jordan is having another party this weekend after the big game. I think we should talk to Brian after the game," he says as he nuzzles into my neck.

"I thought you were going to break up with me," I mumble as a tear falls from my eyes.

He pulls back to look at me. He wipes the tear from my cheek. "No way. I just finally got you, I'm not letting you go."

"Can I ask you something?"

He nods.

"How long have you liked me?"

He huffs. "You've been talking to Jordan, huh?"

I nod.

He proceeds to tell me that he has liked me since freshman year. That he was going to ask me out at the party we went to, the one that I was... well you know. He said he had heard someone was assaulted that night, but he didn't want to believe that it was me.

He tells me that he noticed I didn't hang out anymore and he figured I was just not interested but that didn't stop him from wanting to ask me out. Some things he remembers about our times together amazes me. The things he has done and said over the years make sense now. I asked him what made him change his mind and to ask me out. He said that night I danced with him set him on fire. That he wanted to kiss me that night so bad that he just had to do something. He tells me about the conversation with Jordan and David that night, the one that I overheard. He asked me if I heard it and I said yes.

He said there was no way he could let David try to make a move on me and after he saw the accidental kiss Jordan and I had, he couldn't let him pursue me, either. Basically, it was jealousy that made him do it. He said he was afraid to ruin his relationship with my brother but the thought of me being with someone else was even worse. So, he texted me, after he stole my number from Brian's phone that evening.

We got to know each other over texting, and he knew he had to touch me again. He asked me that night if I needed a dance partner again, but we never got to. I'm okay with that though because what we did get to do was even better. That was our first real kiss.

He tells me to be prepared during school this week. He said that Brittany is mad he was with someone and not her and she was going to be a real witch this coming week. She would probably try something at some point, but I needed to trust him. I do trust him. I already know he hasn't slept with her and if he was going to, he would have already. Before we started seeing each other.

"Can I ask you something now?" he asks as he strokes my face with his hand.

"Yes."

"Will you be my girlfriend?"

I can't help but smile. "Did you seriously just ask me to be your girlfriend?"

He nods as he smiles. "Yes, I did. You are the only person I have ever asked."

"Then let me be the only person to say yes." He leans in and kisses me. I love kissing him. I can't get enough of him.

We watch the rest of the second movie, with some kissing mixed in. We don't see the witch anymore the rest of the night. Maybe she rode her broomstick home.

Christian takes me home and I see Brian isn't home yet. Good. I just hope he doesn't come home while we are on the porch because that's where we are now, and I am about to get kissed. Christian's kisses make me weak in the knees. It's all I can do to remain upright when his lips touch mine. He laughs on my lips as he holds onto me tighter. I let go and kiss him back with just as much need as he kisses me with.

He told me he was in trouble with me. That is nothing compared to the trouble I'm in. I'm falling for this guy and I hope he feels the same way.

CHAPTER TWELVE

AFTER THE BIG GAME

The next week at school was good. So far Brittany hasn't started any issues. She has been around but hasn't tried to touch him anymore. I would like to think that she has given up, but that isn't her nature.

We filled James in on everything and he said he would watch out for her, too. I finally told Jenny today and that we were going to tell Brian tonight, after the game. She congratulated me and said she thought we were getting awfully close. We have had several stolen moments throughout the week. One day I was walking past a closet and was pulled inside. I was met with my boyfriend's lips on mine and his hands on my ass. No complaints here, other than when he stopped kissing me. I have given up on lip gloss this week because he ends up wearing more of it than I do, and I am not sure pink berry is his color.

Tonight is the game and I'm talking to our group. It's Sadie, James and I with Brian, Jenny, Jordan, David, and

Christian. David and Brian have made up. That gives me hope.

Tonight is the first football game I don't sit with my friends in the deserted part of the stands. Instead, we all sit closer to the field. We are behind the team where they sit on the field. Christian sees where we are sitting and he winks at me. I touch his class ring. The one that he gave me, and I have on a long necklace and tucked into my shirt. He says his ring is lucky to be down there.

We end up winning the game. I'm so happy that I can't stop cheering and clapping for them. After the game is over and Brian comes over to kiss Jenny, I see Christian blow me a kiss. There is so much going on that no one notices.

I ride to Jordan's with Sadie and James like always. When we get there, the party is in full swing. We always stop to get some food on our way. It has become our tradition. Sadie says it helps her to drink and not have such a headache the next day. Either way, we are usually hungry by then. Maybe next time I can bring my boyfriend.

I see Brian and Jenny in their usual spot and Jordan is close by. I'm assuming that Christian has already told him that we were telling Brian tonight and after the David thing, he wanted to be close by. I'm a little nervous about it, but I think we'll be okay. I hope so anyway. I get a text and I take my phone out to see my baby has messaged me.

Sam: Hey, baby. You here yet?

Yes, I still have him under Sam. Tonight that changes.

Me: Just got here.

Sam: You still at the cars?

Me: Yes.

Sam: Meet me in the barn?

Me: Okay.

I tell James and Sadie that I'm going to the barn for a minute. I'll be over there in a few minutes.

They smile knowing who I'm meeting.

I walk into the barn and as soon as I do someone grabs my wrist and pulls me into the first stall.

"Hi, baby," he whispers before his lips are on mine. He doesn't even give me a chance to answer.

I don't mind one tiny little bit. When he finally pulls back, I have to laugh.

"What's so funny?"

"Nothing," I smirk. "I love it that you wanted to kiss me so bad."

"Then you will love this," he says as he picks me up. I wrap my legs around his waist to hold onto him. He backs me up against the wall and his lips are on mine again. His hands are on my ass, holding me in place. He grinds his hips into mine. I can feel him and what always happens to him when we kiss like this. I don't think I'm going to be able to hold back much longer. I know I want him to be my first and he wants that, too. I think I was just waiting to make it official and public knowledge that we were together first. And that's happening tonight. Each time we kiss, we get closer and closer to going all the way. I know that I turn him on, I can feel it pressed against me right now. He does the same thing to me. I never thought I would be willing to have sex with someone that I have only been with a few weeks, but it feels like so much longer. I guess that's because we have known each other for so long. Most of our lives, actually.

"We tell him tonight?" he asks as he pulls back from our kiss.

I nod.

"Good, then I can finally kiss you any damn time I want."

I laugh. I know he's serious and I'm excited about that, too, but the look on his face is just too cute. He is so frustrated.

He finally puts me down and kisses me one more time. "I'm not sure how much longer I can keep from taking you," he hugs me. "I'm trying but it is so damn hard." I giggle. He gets what he said and he laughs, too. "I wasn't talking about that, but since you mention it, yeah it is." We both laugh at his corny self.

He lets me walk out of the barn and he waits a few minutes. He said it's to keep from being seen but I know he needs a few minutes to let things go down again. I love having this effect on him.

I make it out and find Sadie. She smiles at me. Of course, she knows. The smile on my face alone tells it all. I grab a drink and sit with the rest of the group. Christian finally comes out and he grabs a drink, too. He comes over to stand near me and I smile at him. I just want him beside me, where I can snuggle with him like Jenny and Brian get to do. Soon, I remind myself.

Jordan calls Christian over to ask him about something. They are standing there talking when I see Brittany walking over to them. I guess she waited until now to make a move on him. I guess she remembers his girl is always at the parties and she wanted to wait for a more specific audience.

I see the look of worry on his face as she approaches. I was never territorial before but I also never had something worth fighting for before Christian. This girl had better watch herself. I grew up only one of two girls with a bunch of guys. I know how to fight and I will beat her ass if she tries something with him in front of me. After that night, I even took some real defense lessons. I am good at it after the last four years.

I watch her as she makes her way right up beside Christian. I see the look on Jordan's face, as well. He knows I will beat her ass. I have hit him more than once and he knows that shit hurts. He has been a good sparring partner over the years.

Christian looks right at me when Brittany steps up beside him. I can't hear what she is saying but I hear him tell her he has a girl and he isn't interested. I can only imagine what she said to him. I imagine she offered him a quick hook up. I have just about had enough of her when Sadie grabs my arm.

"What are you going to do?"

"She needs to know her place, Sadie."

"I agree, but don't hurt her too bad,"

"I got it, I'm fine," I say to Sadie as I walk towards them. I see the look of panic in Christian's eyes and I see Jordan smile. He knows what I can do to her. I think he would actually like that. Ass.

I get up close to them and I can hear her telling him what she wants to do to him. That just pisses me off even more. I decide right then what I am going to do. I walk right up to them and I look at Brittany. "Excuse me."

She looks at me. "We are talking," she says as she lets go of my arm. I see Christian looking at me with a look in his eyes that says he's scared I'm going to be mad at him. I'm not. He already warned me this would happen. I'm surprised it took her this long. I guess she wanted to make sure his girl saw her hitting on him, in case he took the bait.

I don't let her finish before I grab his face in my hands and press my lips to his. It takes a second to realize that I'm kissing him in front of everyone before he grabs onto me. His hands are instantly on my ass, his favorite place to hold me when we kiss. His kiss is passionate and hard. His tongue slips into my mouth as I hear Jordan laugh. "Damn."

Christian pulls away and puts his forehead on mine. "Damn, baby."

"Baby?" Brittany yells. "What the hell is this?"

Christian smiles at me, his eyes never leaving mine, he answers her, "Me, kissing my girl." He leans in and kisses me again.

"Your girl?" I hear Brian yell.

Oh shit. Here it goes. I didn't think about that part when I kissed him. No turning back now.

Christian pulls me around behind him and stands in front of me, between Brian and me.

"Yes. She is my girl."

"What the fuck? You're fucking my sister?" Brian yells. Jordan also steps up beside Christian to protect me.

"Not that what we do is any of your business, but no. I am not fucking your sister." Christian answers back.

Brian steps closer to us and Jordan steps up again.

"Brian, leave it," Jordan says as he stops him.

"You fucking knew?" Brian looks hurt.

"Yes."

"Did everyone know about this little fling but me?" he asks as he looks around.

Christian steps up to Brian. Not threatening him but protecting me.

"It isn't some fling, Brian. I love her," Christian announces to the entire group.

"You what?!" Brain glares.

"You what?!" I ask, trying to make sure I heard what I thought I heard.

Christian takes a deep breath before continuing and turning to face me. "I wanted to tell you, not like this obvi-ously," he looks at my brother and the rest of the crew, "but

I wanted to tell you for so long." He steps up closer to me, his hands on my waist. "I have loved you a long time and these last few weeks have just made it grow even more."

He looks at Brian. "I don't want our friendship to end over this, you have always been like a brother to me, but I choose her. I will always choose her. I love her."

Brian takes a deep breath and lets it out slowly.

"Is she the one you have talked about nonstop for the last three years and been texting the last few weeks?" Brian asks him.

Christian nods, "Yes. She is the only one."

Brian sighs again.

"If you ever hurt her, I will make sure you suffer," Brian says as he walks over to us.

Christian nods. Brian looks at me. "Do you feel the same?" I nod.

"Well, shit. I guess my best friend and my sister are a thing, huh?"

I smile and hug my brother. He hugs me back and Christian hugs us both.

Brian separates from us and Christian is standing with his arms around my waist.

I look up to Christian who is patiently waiting to hear me say those three little words.

I smile at him, making him wait a little longer. He rubs my cheek with his hand.

"I love you, Christian."

"I love you, too, baby."

CHAPTER THIRTEEN

AFTER SHOCK

It was over. We told my brother and he seems okay with it. He did say that he would appreciate no more kissing around him, but I quickly explained I have been seeing him kissing Jenny for years now and Christian and I have a lot of time to make up for. Christian was all for that plan. Brian was not.

I'm sitting on the tailgate of Brian's truck beside him and Jenny. Christian is leaning against it with his back against me, between my legs. His hands are on my thighs and knees and I have my arms draped over his shoulders. Every so often I give his neck a kiss. Every time he squeezes my leg and laughs. It is so good to be with him like this. In public and not have to stop touching him. I don't know if I could have done it for long.

He turns his head back to look at me. I see the glimmer in his eyes. He wants to kiss me. I smirk at him as I lean in and give him a kiss. It's a quick kiss, but the fact that we can do it in public means a lot.

"Hey, no more kissing," Brian teases.

"Oh... you said more kissing? I can do that," Christian says as he turns around to face me. He pulls me closer to him by my hips. I let out a small squeal. His hands are still on my hips as he leans in to kiss me. I love kissing him. I can't get enough.

Brian shoves Christian playfully. We all laugh.

"Hey, Chris?" David speaks as he walks closer to us.

"Yeah?" Christian answers back.

"If you've been talking to Brandy, and did not spend the night with Brittany the night of Halloween, then who gave you that huge ass hickey?"

Damn. I was hoping that was forgotten.

"Yeah, Chris. Who?" Brian asked as he looked at Christian expectantly.

"Uh..." Christian smiles.

"No..." David shakes his head in disbelief.

"What?" Brian looks at David.

"You mean all this time it was her?" he asks pointing to me.

Christian just smiles, not confirming a thing.

"What can I say?" I laugh.

Brian puts his fingers in his ears and starts humming. We all laugh.

The rest of the evening is going by so fast. Christian never leaves my side for long and almost all the time that he is next to me his hands are touching me. The music is playing in the background and there are a bunch of people dancing. I see Jordan approach Sadie when a slower song comes on. I see her blush as she takes his hand and follows him to an area where people are dancing. I smile when I see them moving to the music.

Christian looks at me and smiles, "Come on, baby. Let's dance." He steps out from my grip and takes my hand in his. I smile at him.

One of his hands is on my waist and the other is holding my hand. He begins to swing me around to the music. I can't believe that we are dancing again at a field party. It's even better than the last time because this time he gives me kisses when he pulls me close to him.

"Boys like me need girls like you, kiss me," he sings to me just before he kisses me. He has slowed his movements and his hands are cupping my face, his thumbs on my jaw and his fingers under my ears on my neck. I grab onto his arms as he kisses me. He pulls away from the kiss and grabs my hand. He twirls me out from him and back to him again. I love dancing with him like this.

He spins me around so that my back is up against his chest. His hands are on my hips as we move to the music. I never knew he could dance like this. It isn't the same grinding we did the first time we danced. It's so much better. We are having so much fun. He kisses my neck every so often. It's perfect.

I look over and see Jordan and Sadie dancing. She is laughing and he has a huge smile on his face. It looks like Jordan might have a small crush.

Christian

I'm dancing with my girl, in front of pretty much the whole school at Jordan's party. I've never been happier than I am right now. I finally don't have to sneak her away to kiss her. I can finally kiss her any damn time I want. A slow song came on and I just wanted to hold her close to me. I love this girl. I have for years and I think I will for the rest of my life.

Fooled Around and Fell in Love by Miranda Lambert was playing. It was fitting for what I was feeling right now. I pulled Brandy close to me. Her body felt so good pressed against mine. I just kept reminding myself that we were in public and I couldn't do to her what I wanted to. I should not be kissing her like I want to with her brother so close to us. Fuck it. I can't stand it anymore.

I place my hands on her ass and pull her body into mine. She knows when I grab her ass I am going to kiss her. And I don't mean a little peck. I am going to kiss her until she can't breathe, until her knees get weak and she needs to hold onto me just to keep from falling. Her hands are wrapped around my neck and pulling my face down to hers. She's holding onto me because she knows what is coming. I smile at her before I press my lips to hers. I lick her lips and she opens, allowing my tongue in. Dammit, she has me wanting so much more when she sucks on my tongue. Holy shit. I'm not sure she knows what she's doing to me right now. I pull back and move my lips to her neck, just below her ear. I nibble and kiss all the way down her neck until I reach her shoulder. I hear her let out the tiniest of moans. Damn, that made me as hard as a rock. I want to hear that moan more and in private.

"Baby?" I whisper as I kiss back up to her ear.

"Mm," she moans in reply.

She must stop that or I am going to have to take her somewhere else.

"I want you." She pulls back and looks me right in the eye. I place one hand on her face and she leans into my touch. "I need you," I groan.

She smiles at me. "Then what are you waiting for?" I look at her again to see if she means what she is saying. I want to take her. I know of just the spot. It isn't too far from here but far enough it's private and where no one will find us or hear us.

She opens her eyes and looks right at me again. "Take me, Christian." I can't help but smile at her. Is she asking me to take her now?

"Are you sure?" I ask her as I feel myself getting even more excited at the thought of touching her, holding her, making love to her.

She nods, "Yes. I want you, too."

I chuckle as I reach down and grab her and throw her over my shoulder, and she squeals. "Christian!" A few people look over at us and my clear caveman behavior. I don't care. I don't care who sees or who knows because I'm taking her away from all of them. She's mine and she just told me to take her.

B*randy*

I'm over his shoulder and a few of the others laugh as he starts to walk away.

Brian yells after us, "Hey, where are you two going?"

"I need some alone time with my girl," Christian answers as he laughs and slaps my ass. I giggle as he walks past Brian, Jenny, Jordan, and Sadie.

"Get it, girl," Sadie laughs.

"Fuck her good, Chris," Jordan yells.

My face is bright red. Partially from hanging upside down over Christian's shoulder and partly due to the comments.

"Don't you dare fuck my sister, Christian," Brian yells after us.

I hear Jenny telling Brian to mind his own business, that I'm a big girl and Christian is a good guy. I can't help but giggle as I get a good view of Christian's ass. I decide to reach down and pinch it. He jumps and laughs. "Stop that," he says just before he bites me.

"Then put me down," I say through my giggles. He places me on my feet. We are beside his truck. "Where are we going?" I ask as I try to stand up.

"Get in the truck," he smirks. "Unless you've changed your mind and want to go back to the party."

"I'm not having sex with you in your truck."

"I know that, baby. But I know the perfect place. It's quiet, no one will be there and you can be as loud as you want," he winks. "Unless you don't want to?"

I reach one hand up and pull his face to meet mine and run the other hand over the crotch of his pants. "Fuck," he moans against my lips. "In the truck, now."

I climb into the truck and just scoot over enough so that he can climb inside. I still want to be against him. He jumps in beside me. "You don't have to do this, you know," he says as he takes my hand in his.

"I know," I answer as I squeeze his hand.

"I love you," he says just before he kisses me. Not giving me the chance to answer him. His hands are all over my body, his lips are soft against mine and I can't wait.

He pulls back from the kiss and puts his forehead on mine. "We can go right back out to the party. We don't have to do this. Even when we get there, you can change your mind."

I start to feel worried like maybe he doesn't want to do this with me. Maybe I will be too inexperienced for him. "You don't want to?"

He takes a deep breath and takes the hand that he is holding and places it on the bulge in his pants. I can feel how hard he is. Even more now than when I touched him outside of the truck. "Does that answer your question on how much I want this?"

I smile as I kiss him again. I only pull back enough to say, "I want you." He moans into the kiss before pulling back. He starts the truck and we pull out of the field.

We drive just a few minutes down the road. We pull into the forest. I can see the moon shining down through the trees. It is so bright, it was close to looking like daylight.

We get out of the truck. Christian grabs a large duffel bag from the backseat and we make our way into the woods a little bit. He holds my hand all the way. We get to a small clearing and he sets down the bag. "I want to stay here with you tonight."

"Okay."

He takes a small tent out of the duffel bag. We set it up and even in the dark it only takes a little while. He has blankets in the bag and he runs back to the truck to get a pillow.

I laugh at how prepared he is. "Did you plan this?" I ask as I see we have everything we need.

He chuckles, "No. But I do a lot of camping and until I started sleeping across from you in the barn, I would camp out in the field instead of the barn."

I smile at him changing where he was staying after I started coming to the parties. He wanted to be closer to me and I like knowing that. He hangs a small light from the tent ceiling.

He opens the flap for me to step inside and smirks as he says, "Milady." I laugh as I step into the tent.

This is it. I am spending the night with Christian. I know he said I can be in control of how far we go tonight. I think I'm ready.

I am ready to give myself to Christian.

CHAPTER FOURTEEN

OUR FIRST TIME

This is it. I'm going to give myself to Christian. Am I ready? I think so. Do I want him to be my first? Yes, I know that for sure.

He takes hold of my hand and helps me to get over the sleeping bags that are on the tent floor. He turns on a small radio that is in the light he has hanging from the top. "Dance with me some more?" he asks as he smiles at me.

I can't help but smile at him. I do love him. He means so much to me. He pulls me to him and wraps his arms around my waist. "I love you." He pulls me closer to him still. "We will only do what you want. I just want to be with you."

Who wouldn't fall in love with him? He is so thoughtful and considerate. There is no one else that I can imagine being my first. I wrap my hands around his neck and pull him to me. I want to kiss him. He smiles as he knows what I want. "I love you, Christian." His lips touch mine. So soft and full of longing. I can feel that he's holding back. Making sure he doesn't push me too far. We are kissing and swaying to the music. His hands are back on my ass. It wouldn't be a kiss from Christian without it. His tongue is in my mouth, doing its own dance with mine. I suck on his tongue and I feel him squeeze me. I know what it's doing to him. I can feel how excited he's getting.

He moves his hands so that they are under the back of my shirt, just above my jeans and on my bare skin. His touch sends shivers throughout my body. "Are you cold?"

"No," I say as I pull him back to kiss me again. He chuckles as he kisses me. His hands continue to move up until they reach my bra. He takes the strap in his hands and unfastens it. He doesn't move in case I want him to stop. I pull back from the kiss and he looks at me, trying to figure out what I'm doing. I smile at him just before I lift my shirt over my head and toss it on the ground. His eyes travel down my body to my loose-fitting bra. I reach up and take the straps in my hands that are already sliding off my shoulders. I pull them down my arms and toss my bra with my shirt on the ground.

I hear him take in a deep breath as he looks at my breasts. This is the first time any man has seen me this way. "Oh, God," I hear him mumble. I smile at his reaction. He trails his hands around my sides to my stomach. His touch tickles me and I shiver. He looks up, making sure I'm still okay with his touch. I am. I want more. His fingers slide up to just under my breasts, leaving shivers and goosebumps behind them. His right hand cups my breast and he stops. His eyes are on my half-naked body. There is no smile on his face, his lips are parted, and his breath is ragged. I know I'm not his first but to see how he is acting; I would never guess he was experienced. "You are perfect," he whispers. I smile at his compliment.

I grab the bottom hem of his shirt and pull it over his head. He only lets go of me long enough to get his arms out of his shirt and they are right back on my body. His eyes barely leaving my breasts. My hands are on his chest, tracing circles around his nipples. I run my fingernail over one and he lets out a hiss. "Fuck."

I let my fingers trace his abdomen. They only stop when they get to the top of his jeans. I dip my fingers below his belt and his eyes instantly shoot up to look at my face. I smile at him. He gives me one of his smirks. He knows what I want. I want him. All of him. "Whatcha doin' baby?" he asks, still smirking at me.

I smile back at him and take his belt into my hands. I unfasten it and go for the button of his jeans. He takes in a deep breath and grabs my hands in his. I look up from what I was doing to see him with his eyes closed, taking another deep breath. It looks like he is trying to calm himself down.

I start to get nervous that I have done something wrong. "What's wrong?" I ask, trying to not let my nerves show in my shaky voice.

He opens his eyes and I can see the desire in them. "Are you sure you want this?" I nod. He removes his hands from mine and smiles. "I'm yours to do what you want." I smile as I undo his button and quickly follow it with the zipper. I hear his breath becoming ragged as he watches me push his jeans down his legs. I can see in his briefs just how hard he is, how large he is. I gasp at seeing how big he actually is. "Uh..."

He chuckles, "What's wrong baby?"

My face gets flushed as I bring my eyes to his. "That's not going to fit." He chuckles again.

"It will, I promise." He takes my face in his hands and looks so deep into my eyes that I swear he can see my soul.

"I will go slow. I promise." That was all I needed. I pull him to kiss me. His hands go back to my ass again. This time he pulls me into his bulge that I can feel pressing into me through his briefs. His lips are still on mine as I feel him unbuttoning my jeans. I can't help but shiver as I know he is about to see more of me. His kissing is now on my neck as he pushes my jeans down my thighs. As his body lowers to continue pushing my jeans down, his tongue darts out of his mouth and I feel it warm and wet on my nipple. I grab his hair and hold him there. Once my pants are around my ankles, I step out of them, holding his mouth on my breast. He runs his hands up my legs while he sucks on me. His hands are in the tops of my panties, pushing them to meet my pants on the ground. I step out of them as his kisses come back up to my neck, my jaw and now on my lips. This time his hands are on the bare skin of my ass. He moans into the kiss while he massages me. One of his hands slides around my hip and stops just between my legs. "I'm going to touch you." I nod.

I want this. I want him to touch me. I want him to do it all, at once. My body is on fire. Every touch makes me want more. I crave more. I crave him. I gasp as I feel his fingers between my legs. I have to pull back from the kiss he's giving me to catch my breath. I bury my face in his shoulder as he continues to edge his fingers in between my legs. One of his fingers slips through my folds and I can feel him touching my sensitive bundle of nerves. I bite his shoulder at the surprise of the sensation. "Fuck," he moans as he steps back. "Lie down." I do it. I lie down on the sleeping bag. I look up to see him staring at me. He looks like a hungry man that has seen his meal. "I want to taste you," he says as he gets down on his knees between my legs. "Can I taste you?" I nod. He smirks as he runs his hands up the insides of my legs. His hands are at my inner thighs when I feel his breath on my skin. His breath is hot against my wet center. He places both of his hands on my inner thighs, pushing my legs open more as he takes his tongue and pushes through the folds. I gasp as my hips rise to meet his tongue. He chuckles as he holds me down. I feel him increase the pressure as the tingles take over my body. My breathing is erratic and I am panting. I feel my climax building as he opens me up with his fingers. "God, you're perfect." His tongue is back on my clit as his fingers rub around my entrance. His tongue is flicking and licking as he gently eases one finger inside of me. My hips buck up off the ground and my back arches. "Easy, baby," he chuckles as he licks at me again. I can't take it anymore. My orgasm is taking over my body. My legs start to shake as his finger continues to enter me. "That's it, baby. Cum for me." That's all it takes, I come completely undone. I can't help but let out a loud moan as I cum all over his finger.

He pulls back and wipes his face with the back of his hand, then he licks his lips. "Perfect," he says as he pushes his briefs down past his knees. This is the first time I'm seeing him completely naked. I'm nervous. I reach out and touch him. He jerks as my fingers make contact, making me withdraw my hand quickly, squealing. I wasn't expecting him to jerk like that. He chuckles, taking my hand in his. "If you want to touch me," he says as he wraps my hand around his thick shaft, "then touch me." He places his hand around mine and moves it up and down on him. He feels hard underneath but on the outside, he is soft, almost like velvet.

"Oh."

His eyes are dark. His lips are parted. His eyes are watching the same thing I am, our hands stroking him. "Don't be afraid to stroke it. It feels good when you do this." He strokes a little harder and faster. He lets out a moan just before he takes our hands off of him. He reaches over to his jeans and pulls out a small foil packet. He rips it open with his teeth and pulls out a condom. He looks at me one more time, "Are you sure?" I nod, breathlessly.

"Yes."

He smiles as he slides the condom down onto his long, thick length. He leans forward and puts his body on top of mine. I feel him pressing against me. He looks me right in the eye. "If you need to stop, tell me, okay?" I nod. "I love you, Brandy." Before I can tell him what I am feeling, his lips are on mine. His body is laying on mine and I can feel him at my entrance. He slowly presses his hips forward causing the tip of him to enter me. I gasp as he spreads me open. He does as he promised. He takes it slow, easing himself further and further, one inch at a time. "You are so tight."

I can't speak. It's all I can do to concentrate on the feeling of him filling me up. He continues to push forward as I feel a sharp pain. As soon as I gasp, he stops.

"Are you okay?" I nod. "I'm almost all the way in." I nod again. He smiles at me as he pushes the rest of the way inside of me. As soon as he is in, he stops and looks at me. "I love you so much, Brandy."

This time he allows me time to answer him. "I love you, too." He leans down and takes my lips with his again. As he kisses me, I notice he is pulling back. I grab him around his waist and hold him close to me.

"Are you okay?" he asks as he looks in my eyes, making sure that I'm okay.

"Don't go," I say panting.

He chuckles, " I'm not leaving." He pulls out almost all the way and then pushes back inside of me. I gasp as he fills me completely. He continues this rocking motion, slow and steady as my body adjusts to his size and movement. "I don't know how much longer I can make it, baby. You are just so tight and feel so good around me." He kisses me as he grunts. "I have wanted this for so long." I feel his body raising off of mine just enough to get his hand in between us, to rub my sensitive area. He continues to rub me as he rocks in and out of my body. "Oh, God. I'm almost there," he says as he rubs me faster and harder.

"Me, too." My back arches and my muscles clamp down onto him as another orgasm takes over my body.

"Oh, thank God," he grunts as I feel him speed up his movements. His breathing is fast, his hips are pushing into me and I feel him pulse inside of me. "Fuck," he moans into my neck as he stills his hips. I can feel him throbbing inside of me as he gives me a few more thrusts of his hips before he kisses me again. I wrap my arms around his neck and pull him into the kiss. His arms are under my arms, with his hands wrapped up around the backs of my shoulders, his fingers coming over my shoulders to the front of my body. He is still inside of me while he kisses me. I can feel him starting to soften as he slides out of me and lies on his side, beside me, keeping his arm over my stomach. He props his head on his other arm as he kisses my cheek.

I turn to face him as he pulls the condom off and tosses it aside. His arm is back over my waist as he pulls my body to his. "That was..." he pauses.

"Incredible?" I ask, smiling at him.

He nods. "Yes, it was fucking amazing." He kisses my lips briefly. He sits halfway up and pulls one of the blankets up and over our naked bodies. He chuckles. "I think I just found my favorite place to be."

"Where is that?" I ask teasing him.

"Inside of you."

CHAPTER FIFTEEN

THE MORNING AFTER

Birds are chirping, wind is lightly blowing, and I have a cramp in my neck. I reach back to rub it and instead of finding my soreness, I hit someone in the face.

"Ouch," I hear along with a chuckle.

I immediately turn around to see who I hit. I see Christian, one eye open, smiling at me.

"Christian?" I ask, sleepily.

"Yeah."

"Where are we?" I ask, pulling the blanket up around my chin.

He chuckles as he pulls me closer to him. I can feel his body, his skin, against mine. I lift the blanket to see that I'm naked. It's then that I notice he's naked, as well. I can feel my face turning red and hot. He just smiles at me as he leans in and kisses my neck.

"We are in a tent, just about a mile from Jordan's field,"

he says as he nuzzles me.

I relax into his arms and I remember what happened last night. My face is flushed and warm. My obvious embarrassment makes Christian laugh.

"I love it when you blush," he says as he kisses my forehead.

Christian pulls the blanket up around us and holds me close to him. "How are you feeling this morning?"

I smile, thinking about last night. I was ready. I wanted it to be him. It was as perfect as I could have ever imagined. "I'm good."

I hear him take in a deep breath and sigh.

I start to get worried he may be rethinking us. I know that I shouldn't think that way. There is no reason to have these thoughts. He has never given me any indication that he regrets us or what we did last night but I can't help it. "What's wrong?" I ask, hoping it's nothing bad.

"Nothing." I can tell he's holding back.

I lift my head and look him in the eye. I can see the look on his face. I know something is bothering him. I ask him again, "What's wrong?"

He sighs again. "I don't want to leave this spot."

I smile at him. He is such a sweet guy. "Are you sure nothing else is wrong?"

He gives me a short and sweet kiss to my lips. "I wish we could stay right here, in this moment, forever. I don't want to share us with anyone else. I want you to myself, all the time."

"I love you, Christian."

I see a look of longing take over his face. "I love you, too."

I see it. I can tell he means it. He loves me. He loves me as much as I love him. I never thought in a million years that I would be lying here with Christian, the morning after I gave myself to him. I gave him all of me. My body, my heart and my soul. I never imagined it was possible to find the love of your life so early, but here he is. I'm not sure that anyone else could ever even come close to him. Not only is he smart and handsome but he is also sweet, caring, kind, and thoughtful. He is the type of man that a girl would be lucky to have for the rest of their life.

We finally get up and get dressed. I agree with him, I don't want to leave this spot, either. I'm not sure I want to share us, either. I want to keep him all to myself. It's early enough that I'm sure that everyone back at Jordan's is up and eating. We take down our tent and pack up the truck. We head back to Jordan's hand in hand. We pull in and can smell the food cooking. We are still inside the truck when Christian looks at me and smiles.

"You're mine," he says as he kisses the back of my hand.

"And you're mine," I answer him back.

We get out of the truck and meet in front of it. He wraps his arm around my shoulders and I wrap mine around his waist. He kisses my temple and we walk over to where everyone else is.

Sadie is the first to walk up to us. The look on her face shows she knows what happened last night. "Well, well. Look at what we have here," she says as she laughs.

"Hi," I answer shyly. There is no use being shy about it. I can tell she knows.

Christian pulls me into him closer. He leans down and kisses my lips. "I'll get us something to eat."

I nod. I'm hungry and this will give Sadie and I a chance to talk. He lets go of me and goes over to the fire where they are cooking.

Sadie takes the chance to ask, "So, did you do it?"

My face gets red and hot. I nod. She squeals and the

guys look over to where we're standing. I see the smile creep up on Christian's face as he glances at us. I see Jordan smack Christian on the back and I see Brian giving him a dirty look. The thing that I notice the most is the smile on Christian's face when he looks at me. I love having that effect on him.

Sadie's still smiling. "How was it? Is he good? I bet he is," she continues. I can't do anything more than just nod and smile. I'm barely listening to Sadie talking when I see Brittany walking up to the group of guys. She looks like she is headed right to Christian. I can't hear what they are saying but I can tell she is hitting on him. She knows he and I left together last night and then returned this morning together. I don't know why I expect her to care about that, though. She never cared he wasn't with her all the time, she just wanted him when he would give her the time of day. I hate to tell her that she is going to have to get her time from someone else now. He's mine.

Sadie notices her, too. "You better go get your man before I have to kick that girl's ass."

I laugh at my best friend because I know she means it. She has never liked Brittany and this is not helping that situation.

We both walk over to the guys and I can hear her talking to him now.

"You look good this morning, Christian," she says as she tries to touch his arm. He pulls back from her.

"Brittany, leave me alone. I have a girlfriend."

I smile at him calling me his girlfriend. I have never heard him call any other girl that in all the years we have known each other. I love hearing it.

"Girlfriend? You don't do girlfriends," she says, stunned.

"I do now, since I finally got the girl I've wanted all

these years."

All these years? I know I had heard he was talking about me for the last three years, but I didn't realize how much he cared.

I walk up behind him and put my arms around his waist and my head on his back. He places his plates on the table and puts his hands on mine. "Hi, baby." He lifts his arm up so he can turn around and put his arms around me. I lay my head on his chest, he wraps his arms around me, and kisses the top of my head. "I got our food."

I bury my head into his chest. "Thank you," I say as I pull back from his chest.

He gives me a quick kiss on the lips before we pull apart. He turns and grabs my plate and hands it to me. I take it and take a bite. "Yummy."

He laughs as he grabs his plate and takes a bite. We eat and talk to everyone that is by the fire. The fire feels good. Even my brother is laughing and joking. He had a bit of a frown on his face when we first got here and Christian was over getting us food, but he seems much better now. I know my brother thinks of Jordan and Christian as brothers, but I also know that he was worried about him using me and then moving on. I think these public displays of affection are calming him down. Christian has never been like this with anyone before. He was never affectionate to any girl in front of anyone else. He is different with me. We are different.

We have a good time the rest of the morning. Other than when we ate, we have not been able to keep our hands off of each other. If I am not touching him, he is touching me. He gives me kisses over and over. Nothing compared to the kisses that he gave me last night when we were alone, but I love the tenderness of his kisses today. He is being loving and sweet.

CHAPTER SIXTEEN

OUR FUTURE

The rest of our year has been wonderful. Christian and I spend as much time together as we can. Every football game, I'm right there, cheering him on. We spend the weekends at Jordan's parties. He never leaves my side and he still must have his hands on me in some way. The public affection has only gotten more often. My brother has accepted the fact that we are together. He's told me since that first weekend he always knew that Christian loved me but he wasn't sure I was ready for it. I finally told him what happened to me that first party. He was so mad. Not at me but because I didn't feel like I could tell him what happened. We never did find out who it was, but I'm okay. I've moved past it. Christian helped with that. No one would ever be stupid enough to try anything now. Everyone knows I'm his and he's mine. Even the other girls have finally backed off. That took a few months, but they finally figured out he isn't going to cheat with them.

Christian and I are both going to college. We both chose the same school. I'm sure we could have handled being at different schools if we had to, but neither of us wanted to be apart for that long.

Today is the day that we graduate college. We are still in love and don't like to be apart for long periods of time. My brother and Jenny are engaged and the wedding is planned for next weekend. Christian said he wants to take me out to dinner tonight. I'm excited to get our life started, together.

"You look beautiful, baby," he says as I come out of our bedroom. We moved in together as soon as we could and have never been happier. I'm looking forward to celebrating our graduation tonight with all our family.

"Thank you."

We head over to the restaurant and meet with my parents, his parents, Sadie, Brian and Jenny. We eat, talk, and laugh. I love it when we all get together like this. We do it at least once a month. This month we waited until graduation night. Dessert was on its way and Christian was acting a little strange. I don't know what's wrong with him. The waitress brings out our cake and Christian isn't saying a word. No one else seems to notice his behavior. I reach under the table and take his hand. He looks at me and smiles. I mouth, "You okay?" He nods.

Instead of bringing each of us a slice, I see them bringing the whole thing. Once they set it down on the table, I see it's heart shaped. There's a pink rose on the top corner of the cake. Across it, there is something written. It says, "All that I am, all that I do, all that I have is wrapped up in you. All our future, all we can be, rests on this precious moment. Will you marry me?"

Tears instantly form in my eyes, spilling over onto my cheeks. I look beside me to see Christian rising from his chair. He goes down onto one knee beside me and pulls out a box.

Opening it, he says, "I have loved you most of my life. It took me a while to get the courage to tell you how I felt about you for fear you would never see me as more than a friend or worse yet, as your brother's friend. I was scared you would never see me for anything other than your brother's crazy friend."

I look down at the ring shining in the box in his hands.

"I love you. I love you more than anything else in this world. It would make the happiest man in the whole world if you would agree to be my wife."

I can't speak. I love this man more than I ever thought was possible to love anyone. I want to be his wife more than I want to take my next breath. He is the one for me. He is the other half of me. I nod my head as the tears continue to fall.

He smiles, "Yes?"

"Yes."

He slips the ring onto my finger and stands in front of me. He pulls me up to stand in front of him. All our family at the table are cheering and clapping, making the rest of the restaurant cheer and clap with them. Christian takes my face in his hands and looks me right in the eye. "I know you thought I had the wrong number all those years ago, but it couldn't have been more right."